THE CASE OF THE

As a young man, Malcolm Noble served in the Portsmouth Police, a chapter in his life that provides some background to his crime fiction. *The Case of the Naughty Wife* is the latest in his series of mystery novels that follow the characters from the 1930s through to the 1960s. Press reviews have emphasised the author's sense of place and atmosphere, his strong characterisation and first rate storytelling.

Malcolm Noble lives in Market Harborough where he and his wife run a bookshop.

BY THE SAME AUTHOR

The Clue of the Curate's Cushion
A Mystery of Cross Women
The Case of the Dirty Verger
Timberdick's First Case
Liking Good Jazz
Piggy Tucker's Poison
The Parish of Frayed Ends

www.bookcabin.co.uk

MALCOLM NOBLE

The Case of the Naughty Wife

Matador
5 Weir Road
Kibworth Beauchamp
Leicester LE8 0LQ, UK
Tel: (+44) 116 279 2299
Fax: (+44) 116 279 2277
Email: books@troubador.co.uk
Web: www.troubador.co.uk/matador

ISBN 978 1848 764 736

British Library Cataloguing in Publication Data.
A catalogue record for this book is available from the British Library.

Typeset in 10.5pt Stempel Garamond by Troubador Publishing Ltd, Leicester, UK

Matador is an imprint of Troubador Publishing Ltd

Printed in Great Britain by the MPG Books Group, Bodmin and King's Lynn

To Christine

PART ONE

1945

ONE

From Old Ned's Yesterdays

January 1945. The Germans were fighting back in the Ardennes and firing rockets at London, Jack Priestley was back on the BBC and, in a small market town in East Anglia, a troop of Yankee MPs were on my tail.

I got away from the Jockey Rooms without causing alarm. I stopped to kiss the red-haired chambermaid (perhaps that was too clever) but I was out of the hotel and heading downhill while everyone thought I was still in the kitchens. I kept the document case under my coat and walked down the middle of the road towards Market Street. "Keep it plain," Paddy had told me, "and try not to look like a highwayman," so I touched my hat and wished a pleasant good evening to the special constable on the steps of The Angel. That's when a fistful of Americans spilled out of The Grapes and started hallowing. The redhead threw open her bedroom window and shouted that she wanted her drawings back and a plump woman with no shoes on her feet stumbled onto the pavement and pointed: "That's him!" I don't know what she said to the old copper because I was already running away but, as I turned into Greetham Street, I looked back and saw him bolt into the hotel lobby.

My Atlantic cousins were fifty yards behind and gaining. They looked all thighs and shoulders, with leather ropes on their belts and baseball bats held high in the air. They bounded along Market Street like old Portsmouth's best press gang.

"Get going," I yelled as I swung myself into the spartan cab of Paddy's old Foden. "I've woken up the bloody Boston Tea Party!"

Before I had time to shut myself in, Paddy had slipped the clutch and was steering the wagon through the old market place. This man had driven ambulances in the Spanish War. He had run guns out of Gibraltar and some people said that he had built midget submarines for Buster Crabb. I doubted that, but I knew he could keep an engine going when there was nothing to hold it together and, on the beach at Dieppe, he had shown that he was just as good at keeping Ned Machray alive. So, six months before D-Day, when Buttermilk Dolby told me to lose myself in East Anglian farmlands and sworn me to keep everything secret, I made sure that Paddy Marks knew where I was and what I was up to. He saved my life again, last Good Friday, when a teenage girl with poison in her heart had tied me to the grinding stone of a Cambridgeshire windmill. The dramatic Easter rescue prompted Buttermilk to put the Irishman on his payroll. Now, Paddy was my field leader and I was supposed to do what he told me.

"As plain as you like, Ned. That's what I said."

"Crike, Paddy. You didn't expect this to work. No-one did."

He gave me a sideways look. "Buttermilk Dolby wants you and the papers in London by midnight."

"Stuff him." We were out of the town and heading south but the capital was still two or three hours away. We were in the quiet old English counties but, with Paddy Marks, every job felt like a foreign country; every time was wartime. Engine noise filled the cab and fumes were coming up from the gearbox casing. "Any sign of them, do you think?" I asked as I rubbed the dirty window and tried to look in the wing mirror.

"They'll have called for reinforcements," he said. "Uncle Sam always has reinforcements. We need to keep our foot down."

Yes, Paddy. Please do that.

"I've always worried about the Americans," I said. "They've no sense of proportion."

Then Paddy let me in on the rest of the plan. "I'm taking you as far as Royston where a priority transport will pick you up."

"Not the bloody Air Force," I complained. I was hanging onto the leather strap on the doorframe and trying to wedge my knees against the rusty bulkhead. God, it was cold. "Tell me, not the Air Force."

"They know nothing about tonight's escapade, so just keep it plain. No story-telling, Ned." Maybe he thought that he had told me off too much. His face came over all pleased and grateful. "We've done well tonight, Ned. We've saved the whole Penrith idea."

"If we get away with it."

He whistled something Irish, then treated me to another sideways look. "Did you say good-night to the lovely Maureen?"

I let him make up his own mind about that. I said, "A long time ago – like, this time last year – it didn't matter to me if I survived the war or not. I used to think , 'This is your war, Ned. Your time. This war's what you're here for and nothing comes after it', so go for the high game and what the hell."

"Aye, the devil may care."

"But now, Pat, you know ..."

"Oh-aye, I think I know very well."

"It must be lovely to have a woman wanting the room to smell of your pipe smoke around the fire. Now, I look at a girl and I'm beginning to wonder if she can mend clothes and cook."

"Well, I wouldn't know a man who can truly tell." It sounded wise, but I knew that Paddy was too smart to go pondering. 'Get on with the war,' was his favourite saying. He looked at me, didn't say it, and I wound the window down to get rid of his beer breath. Icy air cut into the cab. I looked at the passing countryside but, of course, it was all black. We were eight miles from five airfields but they were quiet at the moment. We had heard a bomber squadron take off earlier in the evening and it maybe that other missions would muster in the skies before midnight, but I heard no sign of them as Paddy motored between the flat fields of Suffolk. It was a long time since this countryside had been properly asleep at night. The people who ran the armies and air forces seemed to do most of their work after dark, and any farmer on his way home from his local pub was never far from a patrol or a picket. So, I shouldn't have been alarmed when I heard the sounds of something stirring in the middle distance. At first, it was one noise then another. But soon, there were too many noises together.

Paddy sensed my unease and picked up speed. "Anything?" he asked.

I stuck my head out of the window. "There is something," I said, "but I can't make sense of it."

I couldn't see any lights but I heard the engines. Choking, uneven engines, running over rough ground. Then I saw the grey shapes pop up against the backdrop of the night sky.

"Oh, for Christ's sake. They're sending a posse of jeeps across the airfield? What's up with these blokes? Don't they know we're on the same side?"

Paddy laughed. "What do you expect? We've just burgled the Head of Tee-Nine. Not even our side's on our side tonight."

He was getting all he could out of the old lorry. His bottom bounced up and down on the broken seat; sometimes he looked as if he were standing on the pedals and holding the steering wheel like the helm of a Normandy landing craft. "Hold tight," he said and put the vehicle on the grass verge. She belly-flopped like a whale for twenty yards, then Paddy swung her onto a rough track between the trees.

"You know these woods?" I shouted.

Paddy Marks was at war again. He was singing 'Somebody Stole My Girl' at the top of his voice – just the main phrase, over and over. The battle cry got wilder as he pushed the truck to her limit. In the end, he was screaming like a savage. Game birds shot up from the undergrowth, screeching and thrashing. Tree stumps and branches flashed past. Sometimes, the moonlight broke through the canopy above us but, all of the time, I couldn't see where we were going.

"For God's sake, Pat. They'll trap us in."

He shouted back, "I'm betting the civvie police have blocked the road where this path breaks cover. I'll get myself arrested – hot tea in a police station while Butters sorts it out. But we've got to keep you out of it, Ned. Can you evaporate?"

"From mist to thin air, eh?"

He slapped my knee, sending the truck into an eye-wincing lurch. "You're so good at it, Ned boy."

"The papers?" I asked.

He wasn't sure.

"If I've got them, the civvies will read them," he said. "But you can't get them anywhere useful tonight."

I was sure that the lorry was close to breaking up. Paddy's warpaint had got the better of him and he was throwing her around like a soldier of fortune.

I said, "I'll take them. Let Buttermilk know and if he wants them so badly, he'll send someone to find me."

He didn't stop the lorry, but when he slowed for a muddy bend, I let the door loose and tumbled out.

Forty minutes later, I was trudging down a dark vicarage lane and cursing the wet in my boots. I had my collar up, my hands in my pockets and the Civil Service document case tucked in the crook of one arm. I was expecting to be noticed and had my story ready. There were no streetlights – even in peacetime, the village relied on the parish lantern of olden days. The miniature wildlife, that always waits for the dark, was alive in the hedgerows and long grass. Things for tomorrow had been left on the front doorsteps – messages in milk bottle necks, keys to back doors and out-houses so that early morning tradesmen wouldn't need to disturb the households. The street had closed down for the night but it had no thoughts of going to bed. On the other side of the road, someone was woodworking in a back shed and, three doors up, a mother, putting the pots out, woke the family hen. I heard a woman singing, unaccompanied, in one of the cottages. This wasn't some idle singing of a housewife at her kitchen sink but a practised performance in a front room. She was doing well until she stalled at the high notes – a disappointment that drew sympathetic applause from two or three neighbours in the room.

Although there was plenty going on indoors, the only person who passed me was a flamboyant character with his bicycle. He wore a knitted scarf loosely around his neck and an artist's floppy hat that, twenty years later, would make him one of the most recognised characters on Goodladies Road. He kept to the far side of the lane and he took his time. He dismounted when he reached the village phone box and wheeled the cycle into a leafy twitchel. He could keep an eye on me from there. His wariness was nothing to do with the war; he had always been suspicious of strangers in his village in the night-time.

Then: "Now, oo-oh, what are you doing here?" inquired a country bobby as he came from the hedges of the war memorial. It was a slow voice, rich in colour and old time wisdom. He touched his helmet politely but, make no mistake, he meant to detain me until I explained myself.

"I've lost a lift to London. I'll be looking for a room." I brought my Identity Card from my back pocket and handed it to him.

"Oo-ooh, there's no need for this," he said, examining it with deceptive diligence. "I can tell you're a policeman, or used to be perhaps. I pride myself on that. Being able to tell every time."

"I came out in 1940. I drive lorries for the government now."

"And probably some more," he speculated. His lips were too big for his face and went in and out when he spoke, and he kept his eyes closed for seconds at a time, as if the night was too cold for keeping them open. "Mr Grangethorpe at The Bear will let you a room."

"You couldn't help me, could you? You couldn't sort it out and get me in through the back door?"

"Not without you telling me why, I couldn't."

"Village folk always want to know the ins and outs of a stranger," I explained. "I'm too tired for that. I'd find their curiosity embarrassing. I keep myself to myself, Constable."

He didn't believe a word of it, but I could see that he liked the look of me.

"I've learned that your villages round here can be especially suspicious. Already, the chap with the bicycle has an eye on me."

"Oh, don't worry about that old bugger. He'll cause no trouble."

"All the same." I wanted to sound worried. "Village life, I mean."

"Ah, villages-in-war, you mean?" He started to make a tip-tapping sound, his lips against his teeth, as if he longed to be sucking on a pipe. "I've heard it called sleeping with danger."

"You'll find all the nosiness, the tittle-tattle, the pointing fingers and the tut-tutting," I said. "But, beyond that old country charm, there's a weather eye for any change of direction."

He agreed with me. "An extra touch of hesitation at unexplained commotions. A degree or two more reluctance to accept the first explanation of things." He handed back the ID card. "At least if I book you in with Grangethorpe, I'll get to know all there is about you. Others don't need to hear, you're right about that, but prying is something that we take a real pride in round here."

Small hotels were austere places in the forties and The Bear was no exception. Half the light bulbs were missing, carpets had been nailed down where they had ripped, and little notices, all over the place, told you what not to do. The landlord, a tall linear figure with a stoop from walking around bars with low beams, asked few questions but looked carefully at my reaction to anything he said. "You were in a couple of months ago. Yes, I'm sure of it." He was leading me up the crooked staircase to the bedrooms. An old wooden fusebox, as large as a guardhouse key-safe, had been fixed on the wall above the bannisters. The cupboard doors were open with the little brass key on show. I guessed that the lights went out so regularly that it was easier to leave the fuses unlocked.

"The bathroom is at the end of the landing," he said. "There's enough water for a good wash if you want one."

"Thank you."

"Tepid," he said.

"Oh, good."

"Yes, it was one of those evenings when the lads of the Uptown Hall Gang were practising in our back music room. I know, you'll say I'm wrong. Wrong, to say practising. Yes, I'm sure they were just amusing themselves. They're all gone now. The whole American Band of the Allied Armies has been posted to Europe."

He took me into a small bedroom at the front of the house. "Now, I've serviced the black-out but your window won't open, even in daylight, so please don't force it in the morning. I'll ask Marcia to build a fire in the grate while you're taking supper."

"No please. I just want to bed down. No disturbance, if you can help it."

"Oh. Oh, so be it. Of course, the price I agreed with the constable does rely on your taking food and a beer with us."

"Well, perhaps later."

"I'm wrong when I say all the lads have been drafted. Half a dozen got left behind and they'll be in tonight, playing on their clarinets and our piano. Mind, I don't think they were properly in the band. I reckon I can see a bus driver and a couple of mechanics amongst them but they still turn out a fair tune. Maybe, as you say, you'll be down to see them later on."

I told him that I preferred the RAF's Dance Band Number One, hoping that the prospect of disagreement would bring an end to the conversation. When he looked ready to continue, I added, "Especially the trombonist, George Chisholm."

As he was leaving, he said, "Good news about Mr Miller. His boys say he's been taken prisoner. Which is a far better deal than we were all thinking."

"Good God, that's dreadful. I hadn't heard. I mean they were on the BBC just this afternoon." (Maureen and I had been humming along with them as we sliced the runner beans.)

Grangethorpe had already closed the door and was striding along the landing before I realised that he wasn't talking about Jimmy Miller, lead vocalist with the RAF Band. No, of course not. He meant the American Mr Miller. "You're a wet bugger, Machray," I said to myself. "Get your mind back on the job."

First thing: I hid the document case behind a chest of drawers. That bothered me, so I got it out again and placed it on the bed where I could see it. The papers weren't secret but their loss would cause a few red faces in Admiralty boardrooms. If I had been followed to The Bear, then I should expect a creeper to steal them back before morning.

Next thing: I pulled myself out of the filthy clothes and dried my feet on the bottom blanket from the bed. More than taking a wash, I wanted to get warm, so the other blanket and the eiderdown came off the mattress and I cocooned myself in an armchair. Staring at the brief case. Keeping the warmth in. Not thinking of anything.

Then I heard the first of our planes go over and, for the next forty minutes, I pretended to count them. But I wasn't concentrating. The truth was I hated being indoors and alone at night. I sat in the armchair and looked for something to read, but it was an idle distraction. There were a couple of books at the bedside, yet I made no move to reach them. I was more anxious during these first weeks of '45 than I had been during four years of war. I was out of London, thank God, but these new death rockets were so indiscriminate and downright powerful (I mean, really deafeningly powerful), that I knew better than to give myself time to think about them. Although they were aimed at the capital, they were pretty wayward. During the past couple of nights, buzz-bombs had struck these Eastern counties but buzz-bombs were different; you could hear them progress over the countryside. The death rockets were instant. You didn't know which breath was your last. (Years later, I spoke to a merchant seaman who couldn't sleep in his cabin for fear that a 'tin fish', unseen and unheard, might strike the ship's hull at any moment. It was the same anxiety that I felt with the V2s.) I wasn't frightened -I knew how that felt- but I was twitchy. Sitting there, with nothing to do but guard a canvas brief case, I started to fidget. I started to check if I was getting hot and sweaty.

I knew that I could settle myself if I moved about and I did that, clapping my hands as I walked around one side of the bed, then the other. Better still, if I could be with other people. That's when I realised that Grangethorpe had left me without a key to my room. I decided that it would be better if I stayed in the room after all, but as soon as I got comfortable again I realised that I wouldn't last more than half an hour on my own. I would get the shakes. I left the bedroom, hurried along the landing and, at the top of the stairs, stowed the document case in the wooden fuse-box, pocketing the key as I reached the ground floor.

I met Grangethorpe in the passage between the cellar and the saloon. "Oh don't worry. I've left you a mild on the bar. You supup while I nip to lock your room. I'll be straight back down here with your key."

I watched him as far as the staircase. He passed the fuse-box without a second thought and I heard his footsteps progress steadily along the landing. Then I picked up the beer and walked to the back room where the American lads were trying some simple swing. The room was as small as a poor miner's kitchen. A skinny youth with a crew cut of blonde hair, no older than nineteen, sat at the piano with his back to the door. Two others leant against some tall stools; they played clarinet and a saxophone. And a trombonist, by the window, was trying to keep up. He could only manage a note or two in every phrase, but it sounded good. I noticed that an intricate crest had been recently engraved on the side of the trombone but the young musician was so lacking in confidence that he kept his back to me, much of the time, and I couldn't get a good look at it. Alright, they weren't the real Uptown Hall Gang. Perhaps, as Grangethorpe had suggested, they were the bus driver and maintenance men who had got left behind. But their jazz was good enough for me.

I stayed longer than I meant to. Grangethorpe was quickly back with my key ("It's all locked up now, Mr Machray") and another couple of beers warmed me through. As soon as the boys realised that I was there to listen, they started to include me. Repeating phrases that I responded to. Extending the choruses that got my feet tapping. Hey, what did I know about jazz? I couldn't play a note (and I wasn't invited to try) but I found a floorboard that creaked and I managed to put my weight on it at the right moments. On one occasion I was confident enough to suggest that they played 'Chicken Reel'. "I heard you play it on the Midland Road last August." No-one interrupted me to say that I had heard some other band, not theirs. Play it, they did. Well, the introduction and one verse.

This wasn't the first class jazz sextet of Glenn Miller's American Band of the AEF, but they spoke of Mel Powell and Ray McKinley so easily (and with so little reverence) that I was sure that they were part of the outfit. Grangethorpe said that these boys had rehearsed with the big band, and I believed him.

It was close to midnight when I went upstairs. I was a little light-headed and I was keeping a hand to the wall as I stepped, pom-de-pomming, along the landing. But I stopped singing when I put the key in the bedroom door. It was already unlocked.

I pushed it open but stayed on the threshold. A woman in beige clothes and posh shoes was sitting in the armchair and I wanted to be sure that she hadn't brought a couple of snowdrops to arrest me.

"Oh, please do stop acting like a Saturday boy who's had his paw in the till. Come in, Edward. I'm quite alone."

She had the document case at her feet. She hadn't opened it. Instead, she was holding three yellow flimsy sheets in her hands. It was government stationery. "The Americans have relieved Bastogne. Good news. I never like to hear of soldiers cut off from their fellows. It's not what they join for."

She was a Chief Constable's daughter and people said that she was going to marry another one as soon as the war ended. I'd seen her before, but only from a distance because, although she was barely ten years out of school, she was already high up in spy-catching circles. She was, just a bit, toffee-nosed. People were already calling her Lady Brenda, although it would be years before she took the title. Some disgruntled gentlemen in clubs said that there had to be royalty in her family, but I couldn't see that, unless the connection was so far back that the colour of her blood was no longer very different from mine. It didn't matter, neither did her mother's marriage or her lah-di-dah education. She was doing well because she was good at her job.

Intelligence in those days worked in streams. (I suppose it still does because I can't think of another way that would work.) The different lines of business were supposed to share and support but co-operation generally meant keeping a wide berth rather than working together. Buttermilk, Marks and I didn't work in the same intelligence stream as Lady Brenda – and that meant that we always toiled against a feeling that we were signed up to the wrong team.

"You're staring, Edward, and in rather a grubby way. Please, do work at being a rogue without being grubby. Slip-shod would do, but not grubby."

You can always tell class. They keep their hands still when they talk. Alright, she was out of my league but, make no mistake, Lady Brenda was heart-stoppingly attractive. Seeing her was like noticing the best tasting cake on a Sunday tea table where too many other boys would have whiter bibs, sharper cuffs and more deserving table manners.

I dithered at the door. "How did you find it?"

"Oh, Edward. When I looked the first time, the fuse cupboard was open and the key was in the door. When I looked again, the cupboard was locked and the key had gone. Edward, it was at the top of the stiarcase. It wasn't difficult to spot."

Had I really made it that easy?

"You're not going to ask any tiresome questions, are you?" she sighed. "Like, how did I know that you were here and how did I get in? Or, how do we always know what you are going to do next? Even, 'what are you going to do with me?' would be a little wearisome but I suppose I could put up with it. You had better ask."

I knew that she was going to tell me anyway, so I kept quiet.

She looked down at the case. "Now that I've recovered the papers, I'm content for you to spend the night here and make your way to London in the morning. My employer is not an ungenerous man. Please, inform Buttermilk Dolby that we shall say no more about the matter."

"Not so fast," I said with phoney confidence. "You lot have tried to sabotage our Project Penrith. There," I pointed to the document case, "it's all written down. Oh, no. Let's have an inquiry."

Lady Brenda smiled. "Oh no, Mr Machray, let's not."

PART TWO

The Twinwood Trombone Murder

TWO

"They're Calling it Murder"

15 December 1966

The night the Hoboken burned, I was upstairs with two girl soldiers. They'd stolen Constable Dickin's trombone and he'd sent me to get it back. He'd wait in the van, he'd said.

"We haven't got it!" Bernice called with the bathroom door open. She had that hint of a Welsh accent that girls from the border can touch when they want to up the voltage.

I was sitting on the bed with Alice, catching Bernie's reflection in the dressing table mirror as she bobbed about at the washbasin. She had no clothes on. I had walked into the room as the girls were changing out of their uniforms and they'd carried on, sure that I would feel uncomfortable and leave. I tried to switch the embarrassment to them by getting a good eyeful, but they just thought that was funny and I was left more red-faced and fidgety.

Alice was down to her bra and stockings and sitting cross-legged on the mattress. "Yeah, we ain't got it." Then her eyes blinked in an odd way but I thought it was a nervous tick. I liked Alice (I didn't like her sergeant). Alice was lightweight and pale and had fine brown hair that never stayed in place. I guessed that she would always have trouble on parade. She wasn't a girl for a boy to fuss over but, if he was walking with Alice along the cliffs, he'd need to be there to catch her in a strong wind. "We was doing what we was told," she was saying. "The Commodore says the trombone is

'National Importance' and we has to grab it before your inspectors go and loses it for good."

Then she gave in to a tickly cough. I heard the music stop downstairs and the floor at our feet was thumping with the noise that a pub makes in a rumpus. But I wasn't alarmed.

Bernice came in from the bathroom, holding a towel to her front. "That's the score, Ned-baby. If you want your trombone back, ask the Navy." That's when she noticed the grey smoke seeping beneath the door.

"Don't open it!" I shouted.

I remember Alice asking, "You and Mr Dickin? Does your bosses do the buses? Are they that sort of inspectors?" and Bernice threw a dress at her, I think, and said, "Get that on, you daft cow. The pub's on fire!" But the panic had already got the better of me and I wasn't sure what was said.

I ran to the window.

"Don't open that either!" yelled Bernie.

Alice had her face in her dress and was trying to get her arms in the right places. She trod blindly about the carpet, yelping like a show-off teenager when she stumbled over furniture or bounced her hips and shoulders on the walls. Bernie ran back to the bathroom, soaked the towel and laid it over her head so that all she had on was this sopping mob-cap. "My pyjamas," she said to herself and knelt at her suitcase in the corner. But all this seemed like girlie stuff to me. The house was burning down and the women wanted to waste time 'getting ready.' Everything in me said that we had to get out. I picked up a chair and threw it at the window.

The door burst open – a crack like a shot – and fire flashed across the top half of the room. We dropped down to the carpet, beaten by an instant, swingeing heat. We couldn't do a thing. We tried to stare at one another but our three pairs of eyes grew more distant. Arms lifted in slow motion. I couldn't stop thinking about faces melting like images on celluloid. 'Burned alive,' I whispered in my head. 'We're going to be burned alive.' The fire consumed everything, not just what it burned. It used up all the noise in the room so that there was none left for us to make. We couldn't look anywhere without it hurting. Time seemed to be sucked away – each second had to stretch to reach the next one but then disappeared and couldn't be counted. We didn't know how long things were taking or remember the order in which they happened. Then Bernice barked, "We're going to get out of here!" and that brought us to action.

"The wardrobe," I pointed. "Bash through it."

I knew that the built-in cupboards were back to back and only plasterboard divided us from the next room. Alice was still trying to put on her dress but couldn't. I was rocking, but my trouser seat wouldn't be persuaded from its patch of carpet. Bernie had buttoned the front of her pyjama jacket. That would do; she'd go without the legs. She understood what I wanted her to do. She crabbed to the wardrobe, got her bare legs inside and started to kick at the panel.

"We're on fire," I whimpered and Alice gave me a dirty look. She didn't think I'd make a good soldier.

The floor shook violently. I knew that things were collapsing downstairs and I was scared that the building would tear apart, throwing us into the pit of a cauldron. Bits and pieces were falling from the ceiling. The whole of one wall was on fire. Something went 'pop' – almost, an innocent sound – then the air was infested with orange and red flecks. I managed to move in close with Alice. Together, we dragged ourselves across the carpet.

"Lost forever," I moaned.

Alice spat an obscenity at me. Our faces were locked for a few seconds as I tried to take it in. I heard her say, "You're a waste." Then she turned away, spitting other rude words about me.

Bernice, thank God, had already broken through to the next bedroom. The back panel was in fragments with flimsy wallpaper hanging off in long curled-up fingers. She had pushed herself through the hole and now she was reaching back for any arm or leg that we could offer.

"I'm with you, Serge," Alice kept repeating. Once guided, she crawled through without help. But I was a liability. I had no strength left and the women had to take one arm each and pull for all they were worth. The jagged edges ripped my shirt and trouser pockets and my elbows were bleeding before I escaped the blazing Room Number Four.

I had done all that I could manage. I lay on the dirty Hoboken carpet, too sore to cough, too sickly to lift my head. I watched the girls drag a chest of drawers to the middle of the room. They stacked a laundry basket on top and a bathroom chair on top of that. I could see that Bernice meant us to reach for the loft hatch. Smoke was billowing through the hole in the wardrobe. I knew I could win us more time if I packed it with bedding. But I lay and watched and did nothing. Alice's swear words were hurting, out of all proportion. "There was no need for it," I kept whispering but I was the only one who listened. I felt that if I could just take a few minutes to cry myself out, if I could just let things carry on around me while I came to terms with all that had happened, perhaps then I would think up some ideas.

Long limbed and roasted red, the WRAC sergeant stood over me. She folded her arms, raising the hem of her pyjamas and putting everything important on show. "We've less than a minute to get out," she said. "We can't pull you through, you're too heavy, but we can get underneath you and push you up. You'll need to help. If you don't help, I'm going to leave you here."

We could hear things toppling over in our old room. In here, the air was getting more poisonous every second.

"Can't we try the window?" I asked weakly.

"Don't be daft." Her stern, disciplined face and blatant feminity gave an uncompromising message: 'I'm in charge here. I'll get you to safety but you do as you're told.'

That's when I heard a low trembling roar outside, like the belly groan that a football crowd gives to a near miss. For the first time, I was conscious of things going on elsewhere. No-one would be looking for us because we hadn't been seen in the bar and the girls hadn't booked in for the night. But, thank God, other people were being saved. Rescuers were about. Fire engines would be coming.

The girls helped me more than they promised. They got me in the right position, lodged my weight where they could suffer it and made all the right noises to encourage me from the uncertain stack of furniture to the stronghold of the roof beams.

The fire had taken hold in the bedroom but the girls had a new strength now. They worked together and, although the flames were just inches behind them at the last moments, their effort was enough.

Even with the hatch back in place, the loft was no sanctuary. The air was baked and full of hot dust and fibres. There was no space to breathe and, for the first time, I realised that we could suffocate before we burned. The beams and spars were hot to touch and the whole bear-trap was as black as the deepest dungeon. We couldn't see a thing. We had to touch one another all the time or we'd be lost.

"Roof tiles are easy," I coughed. I stretched two palms to the last barrier between us and the fresh air. I screamed. The tiles might just have been drawn from a furnace – they took the skin from my hands.

The girls said nothing. I heard them angle an iron bar into the crevice between two tiles. They twisted, and half a dozen cracked and fell towards the guttering. The scent of breathable air drew me on. My back, arms and legs, and shoulders ached but, this time, they didn't scream for relief. Alice first, me in the middle and Sergeant Bernice last, we clambered out to the night sky. The tiles were still too hot to sit on, or stand or kneel on without moving, but the air felt good enough to keep us alive.

I kept myself apart from the WRAC pair. I wanted to cry; I felt so sorry for myself. I wanted to insist, childishly, that I would never recover properly. I would rasp for breath for the rest of my life and I would never be able to drink, for fear that the tea or coffee would tear the membranes from my lungs. The pain in my legs, which had dogged me for a year, would be worse forever, now that the heat had fused my veins and blood couldn't travel through them. Perhaps, having got this far, I would survive but I would be a wreck. I was a victim, and life was too mean to say sorry.

The girls had stopped talking to me, and my mind was making too much of that. I wanted to make friends with Alice. I could never persuade Segeant Bernice to think better of me – she was too bossy and had summed me up right. But perhaps I could make it up with Alice. I was confused enough to think that there had been a special spark between us. Stupid, because I'd known the girl for less than half an hour. I kidded myself that she had enjoyed teasing me when we were sitting on the bed, before we knew that the pub was on fire. 'Oh, are you going to nick me?' she had giggled. 'Are you going to charge me? Oh, I like being charged, especially by an old bull. Is that what you are, Mr Policeman, an old bull?' It wasn't clever. It wasn't funny. But I began to fancy that these were a few moments that had nothing to do with anyone else. I remembered smiling as she struggled to get into her dress. Even when we had scrabbled across the floor, I thought that there was a friendliness between us. But the snarl, the vulgar unnecessary obscenity punctured all that. 'What's up?' I wanted to say. 'We pals?' But I saw that she couldn't be bothered with me. They didn't want to know me. I felt that I had every right to sulk.

I moved half a dozen yards to the roof's edge and looked over. Reflections of the fires in the rooms below were like footlights on a stage, separating me from the rows of people on the other side of the road. They were looking at what was happening yet there was no inquiry in their faces. They were 'looking at' not 'looking for', so I stood on the roof for several minutes without being noticed.

More than a hundred people stood on that stretch of pavement. Some were dirty and ragged enough to be survivors but most were neighbours who had come to watch. They stood with children; I saw two babies in shawls. They came with dogs on leads (whose every instinct wanted no part of it). Some came with each other, others came to find company so that they wouldn't have to witness the tragedy on their own. They stood with their hands in their pockets, their hands at their faces, their hands wrapped around the backs of their heads. They weren't really talking but, every now and then, an individual would lean to his neighbour and say a few words.

The Hoboken Arms. The pub which had dominated Goodladies Junction for thirty years (and before that when she was called the Dolphin Palace). The Hoboken was burning down.

I felt that I was looking at an oil painting on a large canvas, where the different ambers of a bonfire night had been pasted against a black background, throwing light in strange directions so that walls and chimneys, old corners and alleyways shone brightly where they should have been dim and shaded. The folk looked cold – how could that be when they were looking at a fire? They stamped their feet, pulled their collars and kept close to one another. They were the audience, standing neatly in rows, and I was watching them from a corner of the stage. And, because they didn't know they were being watched, they behaved like couples and singles in cinema seats. They gave themselves away in odd ways. Some had their fingers inside their waistbands, others picked at themselves. And others stared rudely at people nearby.

I saw naughty Baz Shipley – out of gaol, only that week – edge closer to the grocer's wife, and when the wife moved, Baz moved some more. I knew that she was looking for a chance to dip into the woman's handbag, unnoticed. Further along, a young brother and sister wandered away from their parents until a large matronly type caught hold of their hands and brought them back to mother. A stranger – a young man who had nothing to do with Goodladies Road – was waiting to speak with the old woman. He pulled her aside and yabbered into her ear. I didn't like the look of it.

No-one was sitting at the kerbs, but I counted four people who were lying in the road. One man was half on the pavement and half in the gutter. Strangely, the other spectators ignored these people. No-one attempted to comfort them or cajole them or put them right in any way. Someone had placed a donkey jacket over the shoulders of one, but that was all. Dogs wanted nothing to do with them. That's when I realised that these ignored souls were men's bodies.

My God. People have died.

I wanted to say something to the girls but they had crossed to another side of the roof. Alice wanted to climb the pitch where they might find more air to breathe but Bernice said no. For the first time, the girls were arguing over what to do.

Was I the only person who could see that people had died?

So, where were the bloody ambulances and the bloody fire engines? The bloody police? The Army and the Navy? I was ready to call out, but then I saw an ambulance nudge its way from the side street to the main pavements. "The tenders are stuck on London Road!" shouted the driver as the cab doors opened. "They can't get here!"

At the same time, someone yelled, "The Navy's here!" and everyone turned to watch the patrol that was emerging from the bottom of Goodladies Road. But, oh my God, they had a fire wagon from the war; it couldn't possibly be up to the job.

Then a stick-figured woman in a short dirty-white raincoat and stockings the colour of rich tea ran to the middle of the road. "Ned's up there!" she pointed. "Ned, are you alright?"

"Timbers! For God's sake, I can't get down!"

I noticed that the stranger was standing behind her. He looked like a teddy boy who had been made to wear office clothes. He took a step closer.

Then Timbers' face froze. Mouth open. Eyes rapt. She knew that the disaster was about to get worse.

She cried out, "Ned, No!"

The ground grumbled, the building shook and a monster roared from the deep.

I covered my eyes with the scratched backs of my hands and kept my head down. I wanted to drop to my knees but I stopped myself – I couldn't see anything at my feet. When the creaking and groaning stopped, I looked up. Ash, grit and splinters had risen into the air. I watched the mushroom turn in on itself, then rise again. Some of it formed a grey cloud and stayed high up or, at the edges, floated away. The heavy dust and debris fell on us like a blanket. It cleared to reveal a great hole in the middle of the Hoboken. The roof where Alice and Bernice had been climbing wasn't there anymore. I stepped carefully to the fractured lip of the crater and looked down.

I should have been with them on that slope. Instead, I had been sulking, half hidden by a balustrade, as I took my mind through a macabre fantasy about the onlookers below. Now, I stood with a displaced drainpipe like a beefeater with his pike-staff. (How had it got there, for God's sake?) I looked down into the ash and smoke that had swallowed their falling figures. Suddenly, the night was cold. Strangely, the fire had lost its power; it burned in pockets now and when some bricks or wood collapsed, they sounded like weight shifting or wreckage settling rather than a threat of further danger. I didn't move. I had nowhere to go and it seemed right that I should stare into the chasm until I found some answers. Some things can't be moved on from.

Then, through the grey filthy mist, I saw the colours of Bernice's figure being led away by a fireman. She looked bright and white (though she had no right to look that clean). She looked weak but hardly touched by it all.

"Alice?" I called.

"She'll be the younger one, will she?" I turned and saw the cheerful friendly face of another fireman. This one was at the top of a ladder. He didn't seem to have struggled to get there and that seemed unfair. I almost asked what he was doing. He held out a hand. "Young Alice? Is that the one you're asking after? Well, don't you worry about her. She was carried off by one of my old Station Officers. She's been a bit knocked about but she'll be fine."

To me, he looked silly, standing at the top of the ladder in the middle of the night, grinning, like he was in a pantomime stunt.

"You stupid bugger! How can they both be alright? You want me to come down, like nothing's happened!"

He was telling me to take my time.

"You're not even from round here," I complained. "You've got a thick country accent. Thick, I said. I said, you're thick! Don't think I'm coming down when you're not one of us. What are you doing here?"

"Well, now. We've got no problem here. Everything's alright so we'll take as long as we need. Ned, is it? That's what people are telling me."

It took them twenty minutes. Because I was in shock, they didn't risk carrying me down the front of the building. The back wall was safer but something was going on in the yard that they didn't want me to see. Eventually, they dressed me in a hammock and, with a fireman and two sailors guiding me between the ladder and a platform of planks on two police vans, they began to lower me to earth.

Half way down, I caught sight of a doghandler who was standing over a covered up body. The hammock swung left and right and twirled one way, then the other, so I couldn't get a good view of the casualty until I was near the ground.

"Oh no," I said quietly. "That's Archie. Archie Dickin and he's not got his trombone."

I wouldn't let them carry me off. I inisisted on getting to my feet. Still, they tried to scuttle me away but I stared at the doghandler until he felt too uncomfortable to stay quiet.

"It's Dickin, isn't it?" I asked.

"I don't know, mate. I'm not from this Div."

"But he's a policeman?"

He nodded, just once.

"Was he burned?"

"Not this one, mate. Bashed through the head. They're calling it murder."

THREE

On Goodladies Pavements

Hoboken customers had been out in the cold for two hours. Many were too befuddled to go home. Some were waiting for sad news ; perhaps they hadn't seen a particular friend since the fire – someone they had been drinking with or playing cards with for years, or just nodding to – and they weren't going to leave the pavements of Goodladies Junction until they were sure what had happened. Others were lonely people who had to be out of doors at a time like this. But most were good, honest neighbours who came together and wanted to help. I spoke about Ma Shipley; she hadn't been in the pub but had come running and now she had taken Bairnswood Beth and Emily Dawson off for hot soup in her front room. I didn't need to ask about Timberdick because everyone told me. "She was calling you all sorts, Ned. From one end of the road to the other. 'He only went upstairs for a trombone and now look, he's burned the bloody pub down!' That's what she was saying to anyone who'd listen."

I was worried about Tom Ankers. No-one had seen him since the fire, and John Miller, who worked behind the bar, swore that Tom hadn't been in that night, but I had seen him plain enough. And Cherry Red Angels, the Hoboken's best dancer? What about her?

"Not tonight, Mach. She only performs on Tuesday nights and Saturdays. Just the twice a week now."

"But I saw her."

"Couldn't have, my old friend. You simply couldn't."

The barman walked away but Sergeant 'Stand-by' Moreton was nearby. I caught his sleeve. "We need to make a list of strangers," I said. "I saw a youth with black curly hair. Skinny looking. He heard Archie shouting in the pub's backyard. Ask the lady who's gone for the peas. The stranger was telling her."

"Leave it to us, Ned. Just get yourself comfortable." Then he said, "We've all heard about your bravery up there. Damned marvellous. Just damned cracking. Everyone's saying it."

I let him go.

No-one spoke to me about Archie Dickin but I knew what would come out in the inquiry. I had left Archie in the police van. I had dillied and dallied with the girls until Archie lost his patience and came looking for me. Now he was dead, his head beaten through with an iron bar. "And what were you doing upstairs?" they will ask. "Weren't you supposed to be at the carol concert? You were looking for a trombone, you say. But you were no longer on duty, so it was some frolic of your own, was it? A skylark with loose women?"

I watched our Deputy Chief Constable tour the spent battlefield. He wore evening clothes beneath a silk hat and an expensive black overcoat. He was dressed like someone who carried a cane. Without caring for his patent leather shoes, he stepped over the deflated hosepipes and trod into the dirty black puddles where sticky ash floated in the flood. The Dep kept himself erect. Whenever he met a policeman, a fireman or an ambulance worker, he encouraged them with just a few stoic words. If he put a hand on a shoulder, it was to steady one of his weary soldiers, not to comfort him. He had been at many similar incidents and he knew his job well.

I was sitting, wrapped in a blanket, on a white tool-box – not unlike an ammunition box – that had been taken from a St John's van. My back was against the wheel arch and my feet rested on the cushion of a broken car seat. (I recognised it from a cupboard beneath the Hoboken staircase.) The lady who had found the blanket for me came back from the WVS trolley with a pot of hot peas, but my hands couldn't hold it. They were too swollen for my fingers to bend, so she knelt in the road and began to feed me with a spoon.

"My boss won't like you doing this," I said.

"He looks like Adam Adamant on the television."

I smiled and she said that was better. She was a sturdy-framed woman in her sixties. She wore a nurse's cape, grey stockings of many layers, heavy lace-up shoes that had been made years ago and repaired many times by proper cobblers, and a flowing skirt with big pockets and a criss-cross bib over her chest. I knew that she didn't live round here. I remembered seeing her from the rooftop; she was the woman who brought the lost children back to their mother. But although tonight wasn't the first time that I had noticed her, I couldn't place her. She wasn't a nurse because she didn't ask the right questions. I wondered if she was something to do with the church.

"I've found you a bed for the night," she said. "It's so easy for a chap to find himself left on his own after a night like this, and that's the worst thing. Your Miss Timberdick is making up a bed for you in Ma Shipley's sitting-room. She's already there, busy and chattering."

"How many people have died?" I asked

"Oh, don't talk about that now." But she realised that I was too old and sour to be soft-soaped, so she answered truthfully. "Three, that I know of. But others looked in a bad way when they put them in the ambulances."

"Tom Ankers?" I asked.

"You mean the pugalist?"

I smiled at that. I had often thought that Tom looked like a bare-knuckle boxer from the olden days. He usually wore a broad brown leather belt around corduroy trousers, and thick cotton shirts, open at the neck and sleeves, that showed his powerful arms and shoulders. For years, he was known to be the fittest coalman on Goodladies Road. That must have come from his mother's side of the family; it could be nothing to do with me.

She laid a hand on my head, like a mother about to smooth her child's unruly hair. "I'll find out how he is."

I confessed, without thinking, "People don't know but Tom's my lad."

"Now, you're in no state to give away family secrets," she said. "We'll keep that to ourselves."

Quickly, I said, "And I was with two girls on the roof. You'd remember them, they had no clothes on."

"They're fine," she said. "One was unconscious from her fall but the doctor said she could have been much worse. The other had burned her legs but no-one could know how badly. Now, what about you?"

First aiders, with armbands from another age, were helping the bruised and the dazed in doorways, and two ladies of the WVS were taking possession of steel urns, full of school dinners. People noticed that fourteen year old Hazel Day, who had been in disgrace since fighting on the clockmaker's step two weeks before, was working hard with the Trench children. Their mother had been taken off in an ambulance – but how could the kids have got left behind? Soapy Berkeley, in his worn-through boots and ragged raincoat, was searching for the pocket photo album that dopey Mrs Sachs had mislaid. "It means the world to her," he kept saying. "I've promised she'll get it back. It's leather with jewels on the cover." And yet, in the middle of all this activity, I saw a never ending string of silent people with vacant faces and nothing to do. These individuals were in the way, but the busy folk rushed about without bumping into them or telling them off.

The Deputy Chief approached us, gesturing that I shouldn't try to stand up. His lean, tall figure hardly bent forward as he interrupted us. "Who started the fire, Constable?"

"Don't be a silly man," protested my protector. "How could he know that? He was upstairs, wasn't he? Upstairs and the fire started downstairs. Don't talk nonsense."

I lifted my hand from my knee, wanting to sway any further complaint.

"Yes, well," said the Dep. "Sergeant Moreton has spoken to you and I've said that your report can wait until tomorrow. But I don't understand about the station Anglia. Neither of you were on duty, so how did you arrive here in a police vehicle?"

"I don't know. Archie had planned to travel, with the rest of the band, to Shooter's Grove in the bus. I was taking my own car to The Volunteer."

"After hours?" he inquired.

I said, hoping that he wouldn't check, "I had to confirm some arrangements for next week's model railway exhibition. I was the last to leave the theatre, I think, but as I crossed the car park, Archie called me over to the Fordham Street car and told me about the missing trombone. I don't know where he got it from. The car, I mean."

He wasn't satisfied, but I had no other answers. "I'm sure it will all come out in the inquiry," he said. "Now, I need to know, are you up to scratch? A little croaky, are you? That's the smoke but you'll be fine once you've walked around a little."

"Of course, he's not up to scratch," my new friend objected. "He needs to go to hospital."

"Only, people say you should be there when I speak with Dickin's wife. They say it would be a good thing. A nice touch."

She persisted. "Oh, look at the state of this poor man. For pity's sake."

"It's alright," I said to both of them. "I'd like to go with you, Sir." I looked around. "Where have they taken her?"

"I'm told she's at home."

"But she can't be," I insisted. "She was here, on Goodladies Road, when Archie and I turned up at the Hoboken. That's why I went in without him, so that he could speak with Mrs Dickin."

"Perhaps we can mention that. Very gently, mind. She has just lost her husband and is bound to be frail." He stood up straight and stepped back. "Five minutes, then. I've got to find a driver with a car." He inclined forward again. "Well done, PC Machray. You saved the lives of those two poor soldiers. I won't allow that to go unacknowledged."

I let him walk away, then muttered, "He's talking out of his arse."

"Oh dear!" she laughed. "And he's so smartly dressed too."

"I didn't rescue anyone. I was the liability. I wouldn't have got out, if not for that sergeant."

"That's as maybe but you're not to worry about it. They're bringing some more blankets from the Royal Marine depot. That's something we can say about the English. We've always got enough blankets."

"I've seen you before," I wondered.

"Another thing not to worry about. That's a puzzle for the morning when you're feeling brighter." Across the street, a working party of housewives and children had started to unload bundles of blankets from a handbarrow. "Sergeant Moreton's wife is doing glorious work," she said. "She's been here since the beginning, fetching and carrying, making people as comfortable as she can. I have heard that she was first to raise the alarm. I don't know how true that is." Then she said: "Ned, people are talking about a trombone. Have you seen it?"

"Who are you?" I asked knowing that she wouldn't answer. "Who sent you?"

"Was it up there? With Bernice and Alice?"

I shook my head. "I couldn't see it. They said the Navy's got it." I caught hold of her wrist. "Tell me, what did that young man hear? I saw him talking to you, a moment ago. He said Archie was arguing with his wife."

"I've told Sergeant Moreton all about it," she assured me.

"Please."

"He heard Archie pleading that he wasn't having an affair and he was only at the Hoboken for the trombone."

"Before the fire?" I checked.

"Immediately before the fire," she said.

"So, who is he? Who is the young man?"

Before she could answer, a uniformed officer marched up to us.

"The Dep says I've got to run you to Nevil Close," he announced, taking off his hat and going down on one knee. "He can't make it."

"Oh, that's just not fair," my nursemaid objected. "Now look here. I am a friend of the Chief Constable's wife. We sit on the same committee. This man is not going anywhere."

"Well, he can't stay here, madam."

"Then he goes to hospital, or Miss Shipley's sitting-room."

I lifted a hand. "Really, I'd be grateful if I could see Mary Dickin. Her husband was working with me when it happened."

"Very well," she said, helping me to my feet. "I'll get a message to you, just as soon as I've spoken to your Tom."

I sat in the back of the car, hunching myself in the corner and hoping that the driver wouldn't talk. I thought, he's one of the new boys, but I was wrong. I hadn't worked out of Central Police Station since '63 and I'd lost track of the pecking order. I remembered this boy joining the force. The sergeant wouldn't let him near the section bicycles in those days. Now he was driving a brand new Zodiac with the latest siren under the bonnet that wailed rather than see-sawed and made you worry that the Russians were coming.

"Have you heard what they did to the Dickin? Gruesome. I'd say a man gets killed like that for only two reasons. Women or money. So, what do you think? Was the Dickin a secret gambler?"

"Not Archie Dickin. No, I don't." But the lad was right. This had been a vicious killing. It would have been easy to finish Dickin off in the fire where everyone would call it an accident. But the murderer wanted to make their purpose clear. Alright, it was money or women. So, that meant women.

FOUR

The Cheeky Naughty Wife

Odours of cooked bones came up from the glue factory, swept across the mudflats and, although they tumbled and stalled at the high walls and fences of the freightyard, too many got through to the back gardens of the small housing development. People shut the windows at the backs of their houses and they thought twice before putting the cats out. They'd heard wild stories of what the smells could do to a cat's senses.

The bungalows had been built close together in the cul-de-sac. They were semi-detached and each had a concrete path on its free side, separated from the one next door by a flimsy timber fence. The door of one home was only eight feet from its neighbour's. Open the doors and the two families could peer into each other's kitchen.

I sat on the low wall of the Dickin's front garden and waited for someone to notice me. I was coughing from the smoke; my throat was parched and my nose felt full of coarse sand. I was desperate not to swallow it because my throat was already sore and didn't need further poison. I had a feeling if I did too much about the sludge, the trouble would go to my eyes; they were already hurting. I couldn't do anything to make myself feel better. My hands were caked with ash and I couldn't touch anything without dirtying it. In spite of my resolve to let things rest, I did start to clear my throat every ten seconds or so, making matters worse.

I had been resting on the wall for a quarter of an hour before I realised that no-one was in. By that time, I wasn't sure that I could balance on my feet. Then I heard a whinnying cry from the back gardens of the bungalows. It had no pain and no real distress but was , unmistakably, the call of a highly strung woman at the end of her tether. I stood up, steadied myself on the front gate and allowed time for a repeat of the call. This time it was a cackle, like the laugh of a detestable girl who had been nasty to butterflies. I stepped slowly down the concrete path.

Numbers thirteen and fifteen were very different homes. Archie and Mary Dickin's house had the stamp of a married couple who wanted to present a worthy statement, while next door had to survive without being painted or repaired. Next door was cold, Archie's was warm. He had fitted a replica coach lamp to burn above the door and he had bought a deep rush welcome mat for the porch. Plants in pots were in position down the path and, even in the middle of the night, the watering can and trowel, sitting by the fence, suggested that the back garden was carefully kept. Not so, next door. Next door, last Summer's vegetables had been left to die in the ground and old string, once used for marking out, dangled from every post, brick corner and flaking windowframe. A light flickered in the shed at the bottom of the path. An electric line had been run out from the kitchen – when it swayed to the left or stayed in the centre, the light worked. But when it veered to the right, the light went out.

I didn't knock on Archie's door but stepped to the back of the house and peered through the kitchen window.

"She's been out since tea time!"

I turned around and saw a witchlike figure running up from the neighbour's shed. The voice came at me from a long time ago and, when the woman appeared in the moonlight, I had no doubt. She wore a brown cloak, scarves, three sets of loose mittens on strings, and home-made sandals cut from plates of cork. It all flapped about her like the wings of a nutty birdwoman. She kept her head down and her wild hair gave me no chance to see her face.

"Oh Neddie!" she shouted excitedly, shaking her head but never looking at me. "Is it really you? You've come back!"

I stepped up to the fence.

"Thirty years, Neddie. Can it be thirty years?" She put her good hand on the fence and shook it violently. "We had only one time together, just half an hour. No chance to kiss at all, was it? Silly Annie surely said you'd come back. She saw into the future and promised you'd come back to marry me!"

She held out one arm to greet me. The other was withered and bent into her body.

"My God, it can't be you, Polly?" I said quietly.

"Didn't silly Annie tell you? Didn't she say that you must look for me for we are to be blessed." She opened her mouth and laughed loudly, showing her bad teeth and the gaps where she had none. "Poor Polly's not daft and she's not dirty either. I'm wretched, Neddie, you know that's all that's wrong with me."

"I've come to see Mrs Dickin," I explained, but I wanted to say much more. "How long have you been back in the city? I didn't know."

Polly's eyes were fixed on next door. She pointed at the chimney pot, her long crooked finger shaking like she was summoning witches on broomsticks. "You don't want any doings in there," she warned. "It's the house of murders. That's what Archie told your Polly. It's murder in that house, he used to say. His woman sits in there and tells lies. She tells lies!" She pushed her hair away from her face and declared: "Naughty wife! That's what people say about her. That one in there —- she! She's been out since five o'clock and don't let her tell you otherwise. She's not been back. Ricky-ticky-tewing, that's what she's been up to."

"Don't say bad things about her, Polly," I said easily. It felt as if we had been friends all these years and hadn't drifted apart. "Not tonight. I've got some sad news about her husband."

She put two fingers in her mouth as she took in my words. She was older and more rugged but the eyes were the same, and I could tell that she was just as scurrilous as she had been when I discovered her in a pre-war slum, locked in an attic and badly used by her guardians. Something about that childhood stayed in her face. The way she hid her expressions, the depth of her hard and dry eyes, her raw health and – she had already used the word – her wretchedness.

It all went with her ramshackle clothing and her broken way of talking. Put together, they made her a woman who was best to come out at night.

"Don't you want to sit in my shed?" she pleaded.

"One day, Polly. Not now. I've got to find Mrs Dickin and I must sit with her, mustn't I? But one day soon I'll come to your shed and you can tell me everything that has happened to you since the war."

Then she heard the latch rattle as Mary Dickin walked through the gate.

"There!" pointed Polly. "She tells lies!"

Mary was a dumpy woman in heavy clothes. Her dress and coat reached down to her calves and her sleeves left only the tips of her fingers on show. A thatch of black hair – unruly because it was nearly always cramped in a hat – stuck out at the sides so that her ears showed beneath the eaves of an old perm. She walked in little steps, kept her arms to her sides and breathed through her mouth. Over the next few days, I found much that was disconcerting about Mrs Dickin and I allowed it all, but I couldn't get used to the breathing through the mouth.

"At last," she sighed. "One who will tell me everything that happened. People are so kind, but nobody will tell me the truth." She scratched her scalp.

She opened the front door and we walked inside. Then she turned on the kitchen light and took her first good look at me. "God, Ned. Look at the state of you." Her hands went to her face with pretended astonishment. "You're black with soot from the top to bottom. Don't! Don't move from the mat. Take off your boots, then wash your hands. Before you do anything. No, don't! Just don't." She started to march up and down, into the kitchen and out again, looking for something (though I didn't know what) and when she couldn't find it, she worried and scratched all the more. "Stay there and don't touch a thing. I'm going to run you a bath."

I protested, "No really. That's not right," but she was already in the bathroom and the taps were full on. Then she was in the gas meter closet, a broom cupboard, and back in the kitchen with a cardboard grocery box and an old mac.

"Put all your clothes in there," she told me. "Straight in. Don't let them drop on the floor. The mac's for covering up in case Mary catches you when she shouldn't." Hearing her name in that friendly way seemed wrong; we hadn't spoken about Archie yet. I began to undress. Right or wrong it seemed the only practical next step, and I sorely wanted to wash.

She called from the bedroom, "Have you got all your clothes off? Mary will stay out of the way until you shout."

Checking carefully and warning loudly, I folded the mac over my arm and stepped naked to the bathroom. With only a little testing of the temperature, I stepped into the water.

"You'll need two baths," she shouted when she heard me lie down. "The first will turn black with all the bonfire dirt. Then we'll fill another for your deep clean. Full of cream and lotions and bubbles of all sorts."

"Please, Mary. You don't have to. We must talk."

"No, you just let me do my nesting. I'm going to cook you a good supper while you're soaking, and I'll set the front room out nicely. Then, when we're safe and sound, you can tell me what happened to my dear Archie."

But she left little for me to tell. As I soaked, with hot water up to the overflow and bubbles around my ears, she busied herself around the house and called out her findings so far.

"People say that he raised the alarm. He was in the dray yard – waiting for you to rush out with this blessed trombone – when he saw the fire start in the kitchen. He ran through the bars, ordering people out. Next, he was seen at the police van, raising the alarm across the force radio. Ned, I've got the stove door open and a pair of Archie's pyjamas are warming. Tell me when you're ready to come out, but you mustn't hurry. You must soak. You've been through so much this evening and you must take your time. Archie used to say, 'You're never doing as well as you think you are.' He always said that when I was sad. Oh, I should have mentioned that he was talking to the matron, the one who gave you the peas, both before the fire and while it was going. But no-one would tell me what they were saying."

I wanted to object, 'But you were there, running up Goodladies Road. That's why I left Archie in the van and went into the pub alone. So that you could talk together. You must know what happened to him.' But it was the wrong time to argue, so I kept quiet.

She was in the bedroom now. "I don't mind if you piddle in the water," she shouted. "I do that myself sometimes. Ned, you must forgive me. I can't find Archie's dressing gown. He did have one but, you see, he was never happy in it." I heard a drawer drop to the floor. "I know it's here somewhere."

Before I knew it, she was at the open door and still breathing heavily through her mouth. "Something hit him. Hit him from behind, but no-one will tell me it was an accident."

She dropped the dressing gown on the bath mat, and leaned against the doorframe. "I only bought it because the pig next door wanted to. I heard her talking in Widow McKinley's Curiosity Shop. She wanted to give it to my Archie for last Christmas."

"The dressing gown?"

She shook her head. "The trombone."

"I see."

"You know her, don't you?" she asked.

I kept absolutely still. Mary Dickin wasn't interested in my predicament and I don't think she would have noticed if I disturbed the suds that were keeping me decent. But, God, her husband hadn't been dead three hours and here we were. "Polly was a witness in a murder case before the war," I said. "It was a tragedy. She was locked in the attic of a slum in Blackamore Lane. You won't know it. The area's been bulldozed. The man and woman who kept her there used to send men up to see her. She was made to live like a slave."

The story made no difference to Mary Dickin. "Get out if you want to. You don't mind me standing here, do you?" But she gave no sign that she was ready to look the other way, so I stayed put. "They were having an affair," she continued. "No, they weren't. They were having sex, that's all. Every stinking afternoon, twice on Fridays and for breakfast on Sundays. They were going at it like rabbits. The worst of it was, they acted as if I didn't know. As if. I mean, as if. They were doing it under my nose. How could I not know about it? Then I heard her say to Widow McKinley, 'Oh, I must buy that trombone for my sweet Archie.' I thought, get out of my way, you pig. But, of course, it didn't work. I bought it for him and he said nice things but I knew he was pretending that it came from her." She paused, then added (in case I'd missed it the first time), "She's a pig."

"How long had they been lovers?"

"Last Summer....." Mary clapped her hands to her face and ran to the kitchen

I gave her a few moments, then dried myself, turning their fluffy white towel grey, and dressed in Archie Dickin's pyjamas and followed her.

She was washing my clothes in the kitchen sink. "I can't risk these things in the twin tub. They're so dirty, I'd never get the machine clean again."

"The girls in the pub stole the trombone," I said.

"I can't blame them. It's worth millions," she replied, wringing my socks, then dipping them again.

"They said it was of national importance."

"International," she nodded and, out of habit, looked through the kitchen window as she worked, though it was too dark to see. "The whole world wants it. Yes, world importance."

"Mary, you must stop busying yourself. You've got to sit down and let me explain what happened to Archie."

"Ned, you don't know, do you?" she asked, drying her hands on a tea towel with the Tower of London on it. "Why do you think Archie wanted the trombone so much? Why did those soldiers steal it?" She left the clothes in the sink and turned to face me.

I rubbed my forehead and confessed, "Honestly Mare. I don't know what all the fuss is about."

"You mean, you really haven't heard?"

I shook my head.

"It was Glenn Miller's trombone."

I laughed at that. "I've never heard such nonsense! You don't believe that, do you! Miller was a first class musician and a wealthy man. He would never have used an old crock of a trombone like that."

Then I remembered noticing the crest impressed on the side of Archie's trombone. I hadn't got round to mentioning it to him and the trombone was soon missing so how could I have checked it? I remembered the jam session in the country pub towards the end of the war. Of course, I couldn't be sure that the two trombones had been marked in a similar way. The co-incidence was hardly enough to claim that Glenn Miller had ever played the trombone but Mary Dickin saw the suspicion fall across my face.

"Ned, what have you remembered? You think he might have owned it, don't you?"

"Nothing. No, I don't believe a word of it," I said quietly, telling myself that it was nonsense to pretend otherwise.

"But you could believe it, Ned. I can see from your face. You could, if you heard me say it enough times."

"What were you doing on Goodladies Road last night, Mary? You were already outside the Hoboken when Archie and I arrived."

"You can't make me say. Not if I don't want to."

"You weren't at home all evening, Mare. Polly-next-door says you left about six and didn't get back before I turned up."

"I'm going to do some toast on the front room fire." She went in and out of the pantry, gathering the bread, toasting fork and butter on a tray. "Please don't call me Mare, Ned. I've always thought it's an insult. I know they are very proud animals. They look noble. But nobody calls you a horse if they mean to be nice."

"I'm sorry, Mary."

"She was waiting for Archie, you know. There she was, I know, sitting in her dolly-house, waiting for him to park up the street and creep through her back gate. Really! They thought I didn't know." She looked on the edge of more tears. "All the time, I knew. Every time."

"Just tell me about last night, Mary."

"She's sex mad, Ned. No, really. Properly, not like people joke about. She has to have men all the time. It's as if sex feeds her and she has to keep feeding."

"But they didn't meet last night," I said.

She hesitated.

I said, "He was at the carol concert until ten and then he was with me."

Still, she wasn't sure. "Sometimes he called on her for twenty minutes or so in the middle of a shift. I'll bet they called it their quickies."

"And last night?"

"I don't know, Ned." She clapped her hands. "Come on. Bed for you. You'll do no good trying to sleep in the armchair so I'm putting you in our bedroom. You can have the double bed." She wriggled a finger on the tip of my nose. "All by yourself."

For the past hour, Mary Dickin had changed her mind about things, started things that she couldn't manage, left things and gone back to them. I realised that it was too soon to question her about her evening on Goodladies Road. Besides, while it would be hours before she was ready to rest, I was worn out and longing for sleep.

Mr and Mrs Dickin had three pillows each and a candlewick counterpane with a fringe that touched the carpet, exactly right, on all sides. There was a tallboy for him and a dressing table with three mirrors for her. A walnut-cased clock on the tallboy was old enough to have belonged to someone's parents. Its hands were set at twelve o'clock and weren't expected to move. Mary's pink clock on the dressing table worked loudly with the mechanical clicking of a cheap traveller behind a brash face. When you stood still, its tick was the only noise in the room. Six home-made curtains were at the bay windows. All the paint was fresh and the carpet had that brisk look that comes from brushing rather than hoovering. There wasn't a book or magazine or a place to put a teacup. The dressing table had no stool, so I supposed that Mary did her make-up elsewhere. And that was the point: the bedroom wasn't truly lived in. The three mirrors could be set so that people on the bed could see both sides of each other, but no-one worried about that because no-one had wanted to do any watching in here for years.

Keeping his dressing gown on, I climbed into Archie's bed and let his wife tuck me in tight. I sat, propped up against the pillows. I was clean and tidy with nothing to do but listen to Mary's commentary as she prepared the little supper.

"The secret is not to put the butter on straightaway. It's not like toast under the grill. When you cook it on an open fire, the butter frizzles if you don't let the bread cool for a few seconds."

The hot soak had eased my grazes and bruises. The red sore on the back of my calf was difficult to touch but it wasn't really a burn. I was still coughing and my eyes would be dry and irritable for days, but the comfort of Mr and Mrs Dickin's bed promised relief.

She brought a tray with cocoa and toast on a white napkin and sat on the bed as I tried it. "The pig's right," she said. "I went out after tea. I'd got a message from a young man. He wanted to buy the trombone and asked me to meet him at the coach stop at the bottom of Goodladies Road."

"Why did he approach you rather than Archie?" (I had forgotten how good toast tastes when it's done on an open fire.)

"That puzzled me to begin with," she said. "But the answer's simple. Obviously, he had heard that I bought it from the Curiosity Shop and assumed I still had it."

"Alright, so you met him."

"We sat on the seats and he offered two hundred pounds."

"Two hundred!"

"I said yes and said I'd bring it tomorrow evening. Blast it, Ned. I'd had enough. I was going to take it off Archie and keep the money for myself."

"Who was this man?" I asked.

"I don't know. I didn't ask. When he's paying two hundred pounds for an old trumpet, I don't care." She sensed that I was uncomfortable with her answer. She added, "He looked like a Buddy Holly, left out in the rain."

"Buddy Holly," I laughed. "What would you know about Buddy Holly? You've never heard him, let alone seen his picture."

"I have. Really, we've got Brown Eyed Handsome Man in our 45 box."

"Alright," I nodded. "So, black curly hair?"

"Sticking up on end a little."

"Dropped shoulders?"

"With rain running off them," she agreed.

"Light on his feet and alert?"

"Eyes darting this way and that way," she said.

"Like a hawk?"

"I was going to say a tennis judge. Now, that's plenty for you to think about. Settle yourself down and call me if you need anything at all. Well," she smiled, "almost anything. I'll be in the sittingroom."

"Before you go, Mary. Did you see Tom Ankers after the fire? Was he alright?"

She looked at me, puzzled that I should be worried about him. "I'm sure he was taking care of the Salter lads. I'll ask around, tomorrow."

I wanted to fall asleep listening to traffic and trains and all the sounds of our city at night. But I was too tired for that. I had my eyes closed before she left the room and we didn't talk again. Thank God, she didn't kiss me goodnight.

The Dickins had a wonderful bed. I usually had to make do with a civil defence mattress on an iron bedstead that felt like a boarding school rig, and anywhere I was invited involved single beds, uncomfortable for two. But Mr and Mrs Dickin had a wide berth, set high above the carpet, with thick sheets and blankets that stayed where they were supposed to be. Of course, being in someone else's bed, I was determined to be well mannered as I fell deeply into sleep. I stretched one foot into one corner and the other foot into another. I wriggled about and, when I didn't fall out, I wriggled again. I knew that I could roll over and over and not end up perched on the edge. (I didn't roll over because knowing that I could was enough.) I didn't want to think about Glenn Miller's trombone but I began to hear *In The Mood* in my head.

This wasn't a bed to have nightmares in, so I wasn't haunted by a burning pub or the death of a policeman. I saw myself, back in '44, walking down the Midland Road in Bedford looking for the venue where Glenn Miller's band was playing. When I found the place, the man wasn't there. I always thought that he was a phoney after that. Then the picture had me at a quayside pub in '37, listening to jazz on old 78s and, in the random way of dreams, in a Suffolk inn in '45 enjoying the jam session with a handful of young and hopeful American soldiers. Then I imagined the face of a fortune-teller in her almshouse, making up a poem about Ned Machray marrying poor Polly from Blackamore Lane. Now, Polly was in her wooden shed, next door to Mary Dickin, waiting for someone to keep her own nightmares away.

I disturbed at twenty past two. Mary had been to the bathroom and was rustling about in the kitchen before returning to the sittingroom. Matt Monro was crooning on the radiogram but it was low and smoochie and I slipped back to sleep without listening to it. The next time I woke, Mary was in bed beside me.

She had been polite enough to keep her back to me but her nightdress had ridden up to her waist and I felt guilty because I had been dreaming of stroking a bottom and it was probably hers, not Polly's. Her dumpy body had warmed up the bed and the set up could have been cosy, except for her smell. It was especially pungent because it had been trapped between the sheets for —- well, I didn't know how long. She carried on breathing through her mouth.

"You don't mind, do you?" She spoke as if she had been waiting for me to stir.

She kept her head turned away from me, and I didn't look at her when I spoke. I faced the ceiling. "For pity's sake, Mary. Your husband was murdered last night and just look at us. I know you two had your problems but the bloke's barely cold. Grief, I'm in his pyjamas in his bed and his wife's in here with me."

"I know," she said, still looking the other way. "It sounds awful, doesn't it? But we know that nothing's happened between us and I needed to be with someone. Feel sorry for me, Ned, trying to curl up in the armchair with only an eiderdown. My feet were always sticking out. You'd been so nice to me before you fell asleep."

I didn't remember being nice. I remembered wondering if she had stuck an iron bar through her husband's head.

"You were stroking my bottom before you woke," she said lightly. "I ought to have stopped you but I knew you didn't realise you were doing it, so I let you carry on. Do you want to make a pot of tea? I always wanted Archie to do that but he never would."

"No. That would be going too far. We both need to get dressed."

"Not yet." She still had her back to me. We neither spoke nor moved for half a minute. The dressing-table clock carried on being loud and the curtains swayed in the bay where the draught excluder didn't work.

"You still don't believe me, do you?" she asked.

I wanted her to keep quiet.

"I really do have a copy of Brown Eyed Handsome Man," she insisted. "Weston Harts were giving away the top ten with every new television. Archie liked Billy Fury and I wanted Ronnie Carroll, so we did it. We bought a new TV. Brown Eyed Handsome Man was in with the others."

"Mary, what are you talking about?"

"The special offer from the TV shop. That's how I know about Buddy Holly."

I could listen to her nonsense no longer. "Mary," I said. "Your 'Buddy Holly' heard you arguing with Archie in the pub's backyard."

"That's a lie! How does he know? Have you spoken to him? It's a lie!"

"I overheard him speaking to the matron."

She dismissed that idea. "The one who went for the peas?"

The telephone was ringing in the hall. I sat up. It was ten to six. "He told her that Archie was pleading with you. He wasn't having an affair and only came to the Hoboken for the trombone."

"No, Ned. I didn't kill him."

I made sure that Dickin's pyjamas were in place and started to walk out of the bedroom. She yelled at me. "How could you say that! God, Ned, we've just slept together!"

I missed the introductions because Archie and Mary were both left-handed, so I was holding the receiver upside down.

"Connie Freya's broken out of prison," said the Chief Constable's wife. "You're in danger, Ned. Stay where you are until we reach you."

FIVE

In Unfortunate Circumstances

Billie Elizabeth 'Timberdick' Woodcock was running along Goodladies Road, her loose sandals slapping on the damp pavements, her arms folded across her front against the chill. The street was so empty that the sound of her running bounced against the windows of the closed up shops.

Two empty fire-tenders blocked the junction. The police wouldn't open the road before lunchtime. An old constable from Fordham Street had been playing nightwatchman but the site was so wet and dirty that he had asked Maggs to leave his bottle shop unlocked for shelter.

Many shopkeepers had decided not to open because of the fire. The fishmonger's wife was in tears and wouldn't be helped. The Travers brothers wouldn't risk their stock of rugs, cushions and curtains being soiled by passers-by with sludge on their boots and grime on their sleeves. And poor Mrs Twist, who had been selling whickerwork on 'The Road' since she was twelve, locked her door and stuck up a notice saying that nothing would be the same, ever again. There was no music on Goodladies Road; that was rare.

But Mr and Mrs Harkness were up early to start on the Christmas decoration for their leather and bag shop, 'Pop' Hawthorne was standing milk crates at his bakery door, and Bellamy-Drew was sweeping the dirty ash from the pavement in front of his terraced house, as if his efforts, half a mile from The Hoboken Arms, could begin to wipe clean the pictures of last night's disaster.

A curtain moved opposite. "There's no point him cleaning up," Emily Dawson said to her man who, face down beneath the blankets, said that they'd all have to drink at The Station Hotel now. "It'll be days before the last of the ash settles on us."

"Like fall-out from the bomb," remarked the man, Donald. "They say it takes months for it all to come down."

Emily didn't argue. She took most of what he said, on any subject, to be rubbish.

Bellamy-Drew worked on, Mrs Harkness stopped to look, and Miss Dawson let the curtain fall back into place.

When Timbers heard Bellamy-Drew mumble, "What we need now is snow," she crossed to the other side, having no time to talk. "I was saying, the snow would turn it to sludge," he called after her. "At least, we could shovel it away."

Timbers didn't reply.

"How's Ned?" he shouted.

Timbers was running on, but Mrs H reported from her shop's front door, "They took him to hospital. We've no news, but he was on his feet, wasn't he? He was walking." She looked at the sky. "It's going to rain."

"We don't want that," Bellamy-Drew objected, banging the broomhead on the kerb.

"Rain for Christmas. That's what we get on Goodladies Road."

When Emily Dawson heard that, she sat on the edge of her bed and grumbled. "I'm not going out, be it rain or snow or whatever, not with all that smoke in the air. I'll catch a sore throat if I do."

Donald shifted to make sure he left no room for her. "You've already been out, you old crow. You've been up and down, gossiping on The Road for close to an hour and a half."

"Here, Donald Middleton. Who are you calling an old crow?" She stepped back to the window, moved the curtain and resumed her nosiness.

Timbers kept running. By now, her hands were loose at her sides and she had slipped her sandals off. Her cheeks were red and her short blonde hair was tacky with perspiration. Pint-sized Timbers was poky faced and bony with arms and legs at all angles.

On any other day, people would have taken one look at her toy-like figure and said that she couldn't run for toffee. Yet, this morning, she had run every step from her home and she couldn't afford to give up.

Mean 'Soapy' Berkeley, on his way to pick up the papers, held up a hand and shouted, "Half a mo', Timbers! Half a mo!"

When Timbers didn't even turn her head, Soapy knew that something was up and began to run after her, but he was older and slovenly and weighed down by a tattered winter's coat that reached almost to the ground, so he lost ground with each step. As he stumbled over the kerb and into Tykes Alley, a white whiskered mongrel lifted his nose from the gutter, sensed that a game was afoot and trotted after him. A young lad, too young to be out on a tricycle, joined in and, for two hundred yards, the pursuit painted a curious procession, something from a fairy tale. The girl, the man, the dog and a boy. Round corners, across roads, and past windows where mothers looked up and wondered what was going on. A dockyard apprentice rang his bell and waved at Timberdick as he cycled past. Timbers, not wanting to be rude to a regular customer, slowed to a quick march and wiggled her bottom at him. The boy rang his bell in reply, the dog barked and Soapy muttered that he'd remember the young man's face. Then Timbers picked up the pace again and stretched out a lead. Discouraged, (she showed no sign of letting up, but where were they going?) the boy ran out of puff, the dog was distracted by more interesting scents and Berkeley drew up and leaned against a brick wall; he'd catch her on her way back.

Police Sergeant 'Stand-by' Moreton stood behind the brick post at the cemetery gates and watched the awkward figure trot through the puddles. Splashing up and kicking out, she didn't seem to care. "That one never thinks about what she's doing," he thought. Now that The Hoboken Arms had burned to a wreck, he hoped that vermin like her would flee Goodladies Junction. Girls like Stacy All-Night, Black Layna Martins and Betty 'Slowly' Barnes. And that dancer, Cherry Red Angels, who was no better than a common strip-tease girl. But he kept his special hatred for Timberdick Woodcock. Three years ago, when Stand-by was fresh out of his probation but already making a name for himself, he had been paired with an old copper and told to purge the infamous road of its working girls. But old Ned Machray had wanted to befriend the filthy women rather than chase them from the gutter. Stand-by leant against the cemetery post and shook his head when he thought about it. The Hoboken Arms should have been burned down long ago. That's what Stand-by thought.

In 1964 he had been promoted to sergeant, a remarkable advance for such a junior constable. But, this time last year, Mrs Moreton had shown him up at the Superior Officers Dinner Dance. Stand-by had been cautioned about her behaviour. He had lost his attachment to the CID and it was suggested that he would do well to seek employment with another force. "Damnably unfair," he muttered as he watched another cyclist twist his neck to look at Timbers' bare legs. "Unfair, Sergeant Moreton, that you should be criticised. Unfair that no-one spoke up for you. Unfair that you should take the blame." But while Stand-by was out of favour, he saw that the skinny bony woman was doing very well for herself. Oh yes, she was still here, on the streets, trying to run in sandals that were too big for her and a coat that had lost all its buttons. He ought to stop her and make her show him that she was wearing little underneath. But Soapy Berkeley was there to witness it all and he'd tell tales. He'd get her on the way back, he promised.

Betty 'Slowly' Barnes was in trouble. Poor Slowly always lived on the edge of calamity but, this morning, she had dug the hole so deep that no friend could hope to throw down a line. Timbers shook her head, still going strong as she crossed the junction at the top of Slowly's road. This was trouble like Timbers had never been called to deal with before. Even as she ran towards the three-room-digs – on the ground floor of Mrs Ainsworth's; God she hoped the old woman hadn't heard about it – Timbers didn't know what she was going to do. "Oh, not the first thing, Slowly," she sighed as she ran past the empty telephone box. Should she call Ned? But Ned was in hospital, she believed, not at home, and the mess was so awful that Ned would have to behave like a policeman.

Perhaps that was right. Perhaps, this morning, everyone should tell the truth. Again, she shook her head. Long ago, Timbers had learned that it was easier to fib than tell the truth.

Slowly barked,"I've never killed him before!" She had opened the door before Timbers was close enough to knock.

The woman's cheeks, as round and polished as French apples and not far from the same colours, were heavy with tears. Slowly was famous for her crying. She could produce tears for half an hour without rest or interruption, not just tracks of moisture – hardly there before they dried – but good rivers with drops on the ends, as heavy as drips from left-on taps, and bulbous enough to hold their own coloured light. She was so good at crying that she could carry on doing other things at the same time. Timbers had seen this helpless mess of a girl tie shoe-laces, sing songs, and dip soldiers into egg yolk and never let her tears get in the way. But, this morning, she was stony-faced and shaking and staring without blinking. Her hair always looked a mess but, today, it was sticking on end with a stiffness that said she had been scared close to death.

"You look like you've played with the devil, Slo'," Timberdick said, thinking aloud. "Let me in and get this door shut."

The Admiral's body filled the front room. He was bent over the backs of two chairs like a huge bridge of palpy flesh. His big head, hanging down to the carpet, was angrily red and bloated – like a tethered bull's. His hands and feet were filling up with old blood. Slowly had dressed him with her best gingham tablecloth, from the middle of his thighs to the fat of his shoulders. But even in death this male spoke of so much stamina that a frivilous decoration and inglorious posture couldn't make him ridiculous. His grey hair cut short back and sides, the expensive wristwatch, the toughened soles of his bare feet, and even the smell of coarse boarding-school soap gave him power and true hardiness.

"Had you started on him?" Timbers asked.

"Not really."

"Did he cry out? Did he say anything?"

"Not really." Then: "I can't remember."

"For God's sake, Slo! You've got twenty stone of dead bloke in the middle of the floor. Without a stitch on. Without any honest reason to be here. You've must remember what he said!"

But Slowly didn't answer. The two girls stood, side by side, looking. Both short. Timbers, skin and bones. Slowly, puffy and fat shouldered. Their little fingers wandered, unconsciously searching for each other, so that they might touch and hold hands. When it didn't happen, Slowly said, very quietly, "It's fascinating, isn't it?"

"In a dreadful way, I suppose."

"Dreadfully," agreed Slowly. "Dreadfully fascinating. Will he start to smell?"

"Not for a bit," said Timberdick. "Untie him, Slowly. You can't leave him buckled to four chair legs."

"I can't!" she bawled. "I can't touch him!" She covered her face and ran to her bedroom.

Timbers didn't untie him either. She tried to stand still but bobbed up and down on pigeon toes, her two hands holding her head, then her sides, then her stomach in worry.

It seemed wrong that this enormous body no longer moved. She felt herself wanting to prod him with a stick – and, if she'd had one and had done it, she wouldn't have been surprised if he had reared up and roared at her. There was a sense of vulgar butchery in the scene. Dizzy, disturbed and ashamed, she ran to the toilet and emptied every drop of wee from her tummy.

Slowly didn't call for her. She heard Timbers put the kettle on the gas, and waited for her to come to her on the bed. Then she explained, "He wanted me to deal with him before he left for his Christmas holiday. I said, he'd have to be early. That's why I'm like this. I've not washed or anything. I wasn't even dressed when he arrived. I've not done my hair or had a cuppa. Not anything."

Timbers collected her cold hand and held it in her lap. "No, Slo'. Tell me everything."

"It was," she began, then stopped; she steadied her breath, held her belly in and waited for her voice to settle. "Last night, in the Hoboken." She shook her head and started again. "The girl from the Co-Op wanted to play Post Offices, so I told the Hoboken that I needed the back room – you know, the little one up from the yard

– but she didn't turn up. The Admiral saw me waiting at the top of the staircase for her. 'What are you doing here?' I asked. It was unusual for him to be anywhere near without telling me first. 'I'm waiting for my girls,' he said. They were in Number Four with Ned and he didn't want them to come out too soon. Then he said that he wanted to do all night with me and I said he couldn't and he said he really needed it. So, I said, come round to my place first thing in the morning and I'll make it just as good for you. That's the bit he likes best, you see. First thing in the mornings when he makes a mess of washing himself and getting dressed. He likes to dribble in the mornings. His breakfast down his bib."

"Why did you make him wait?"

"Because I already had Stand-by Moreton crying into my lap. He was taking liberties. I mean we don't like cry babies, do we? But we put up with them because we're paid to. But Sergeant Moreton was taking liberties last night. He was crying to me bacause I was his friend, he said."

"Arseholes," said Timbers. "Was he your friend when he nicked you last year?"

"I should have said that, Timbers. That's what I should have said to him."

"Who else was about?"

"No-one. Ned and his girls were in Number Four. The Admiral was waiting for them until I sent him away. Stand-by was weeping at my feet. Oh, and the one Stand-by called the matron, she was asking about Ned. You know her, don't you?"

"Yes," Timbers nodded. "She was in the street after the fire and said that Ned wanted to sleep at Ma Shipley's. What was she doing upstairs in the Hoboken?"

"I don't know. Just walking up and down, I suppose. Anyway, I dressed him in his pinnie."

"Who? Stand-by? Not Ned, surely?"

"No, Timbs, the Admiral when he turned up this morning." She continued, "I made him clean the toilet pan. He was happy doing that while I changed from my nightie to my nanny clothes. Then I told him off and he was loving it, Timbs. Just like he used to in the beginning. He was weeping and snivelling, wiping his nose on the back of his hands and smearing it over his face. Just like he liked. I got the chairs in place and tied him up. He was fine. So I really got going at him. Shouting and shoving him, telling him what I'd got in store for him and, all of it, he loved. Then, suddenly, he seemed to explode inside. Like, breathing out in a great gush, except he swallowed up all the air." She hung her head. "I don't understand. I've never killed him all the other times."

"I'll sort it, Slo'," Timbers said.

"What are you going to do?"

Timbers bit her lip. "I don't know, just yet. I've never had a corpse on the carpet. I've never seen girls do what they do with them."

"They'll hang me. I know they will. They'll say that it's treason because he's one of Her Majesty's Admirals and then they'll hang me."

Timbers grabbed the girl's shoulders. "You haven't killed anyone, Slo. He died under his own steam."

"He died because I was shouting at him," Slowly insisted. "I shouted him to death."

"Besides, nobody hangs anybody these days."

"Oh no!" bawled Slowly. "Don't let them send me to prison!"

"I want you to stay here, right here in this room and on the bed. Don't even bother with the tea. I'll take the kettle off the ring before I leave." She patted the girl's hands, then got to her feet.

"I'm a murderer," wept Slowly.

"No, you're not. And you must stop saying that you killed him. Don't get used to saying it, do you hear me?"

"What can we do, Timbs?"

"Leave everything to me."

"You will move him, won't you. I can't sit here, thinking about his body in that other room. Not like it is."

Then Slowly jumped off the bed. "There's one more thing." She stepped to the corner of her bedroom and whipped a silk curtain from the old armchair, revealing the brass trombone. "He brought it with him," she said. "But he never told me what to do with it. I mean, we shouldn't be surprised by the weird ideas in men's heads, should we Timbs? But a trombone? I mean, what?" She sighed,"If only he had said before he died. You never know, with new ideas."

"I don't think he wanted you to muck around with it, Slo'. This is Archie Dickin's trombone. It was stolen from the fire last night."

"Good God, do you think? Not the Admiral, surely? I better cover it up," she decided, throwing the curtain back into place. "Timbers, we must keep this a secret."

"Just leave it to me."

With little steps, Timbers moved from the bedroom to the threshold of the front room. She remembered how Slowly had asked, 'Will he start to smell?' and Timbers' tummy turned.

"Hello!" she said boldly. But the dead body didn't wake up.

As she hurried past, a fleck of his grey fringe was disturbed by the draught from the door. It caught her eye. Although she shouldn't have, she stopped and stared, counting the seconds, until she felt sick. She rushed to the toilet again and dropped heavily to her knees, hating herself.

Once wasn't enough. Even though she had pulled all that she had through her gullet, making her stomach ache and her ribs cold, she took in great gulps of air and gripped the toilet pan so that she could muster the strength to vomit again. "Go on," she said, punishing herself. "Go on. Go on, go on." All the time, thinking, "Him in there." Him – dead naked, tied up and beaten, just what a hundred men wanted to do to her.

The infant was pedalling his trike along the pavement when Timberdick left the house. He noticed that she couldn't run because she was thinking too much. She wasn't wearing socks or stockings and her ears were turning pink. He remembered that, one day, he came back from watching the model boats and his own ears had hurt so much that he cried. He followed her to the telephone box, then wheeled his steed up and down as she made her calls. He was sure that someone would buy her a new cardie for Christmas, or some nice boots with thick fluffy fur inside.

Timbers dialled Shooter's Grove but, of course, Ned wasn't

there. So she put the phone down and got her money back. Then she lifted the receiver again, but the toddler knew that she was only pretending to be busy because she didn't dial and she didn't put any money in.

She wasn't sure that she was doing the right thing. Without finally making up her mind, believing that she could still put the phone down before the call went too far, she dialled the dockyard and asked to speak with Broadie Turpin. When he couldn't be found, she asked to be put through to the transport garage and asked for Mr Turpin again.

"He's here," drawled the old sea-dog.

"Is that Mr Turpin?" she asked needlessly. "We've not spoken before. You usually deal with Ned Machray."

"He's in hospital, m'dear, after the fire. Is that our Timberdick? What can I do for you, m'dear?"

Timbers hesitated. She thought that he might be making fun of her.

He reassured her. "We met at the Hoboken on a jazz night. You had Baz Shipley on your knee, I remember."

Timbers shook her head but said nothing. Then, she took a breath, tensed her tummy muscles and declared in one go: "I've got a dead Admiral. He died with his trousers down."

"Oh dear, m'duck. That won't do. Any Admiral who dies in that state didn't ought to die out there. Not with his pants and all off. No, he'd be far better in here, in the dockyard amongst friends."

"That's what I thought."

"No, we don't want any stories getting about." He was thinking aloud now. "Of course, it is a bit more serious than the matters I usually deal with, but no, you've done right to ring me. We don't need to tell Ned about this, do we? Him being a policeman at the death, so to speak. No, this calls for delicate handling, this one. One of the trickier jobs that I ever dealt with. Yes, calls for one of the Navy's best lorries, I'd say."

"An old one would be better, with plenty of canvas for covering up."

"You leave the job to me. Just give me the address and make sure no-one else is around. I don't want anyone seeing me."

The toddler had withdrawn his trike to the street corner and Soapy Berkeley was just yards from the junction when he saw Sergeant Moreton commence his striding march from the cemetery gates. Sensing what was going to happen, Soapy giggled like a child and raced into the block of council flats. "He's going to nick her, going to nick her," he repeated as he pressed and pressed for a lift to take him to the top floors.

SIX

The Top of Tullet's Warehouse

"What's this? A poxy fiver!"

Timberdick twirled the banknote between her fingers, holding it high in the air. She twisted it and creased it, wanting it to flutter like a lure to a bird. "Come on then, little Stand-by," she teased, skipping backwards across the road. On any other day she would have told him to bugger off but she wanted to keep him away from the horrors on Slowly's carpet. "Five pound's not much. What's a good girl supposed to give for five pounds?"

She led him on, through Lady's Little Street and along the slabs between the backs of Sutcliffe's factory houses. Past the Boneyard Mission, where Sean, the record dealer, was loading fowl crates full of LPs onto his converted milk float, and into the higgledy jigsaw of dog-legs, concrete steps and cobbled gulleys. They heard people eating breakfasts in kitchens and pouring dirty water down back drains. Dogs were let out. Infants were parked in backyards, out of the way while their mothers got themselves straight. Somewhere, a young girl was crying because the budgie had fluttered out of his cage and might get trodden on. Her Dad wanted to know why she was buggering around with the bird this early in the morning. "It's the girl's holidays, Jim. You must be more patient."

Timbers wouldn't let Stand-by off the hook. "I'll put the fiver in here," she called, reaching down the front of her dress as she ran. "For the time being," she said.

Soapy Berkeley saw them from Nellie Smeaton's veranda. "She was just like our old Timbers again," he would say, days later, when Len, the publican, allowed him to stay in The Volunteer long enough to tell the story. Emily Dawson, who heard nothing about it before Archie Dickin's murderer was caught and gaoled (by which time the story had been colourfully embellished) told the butcher's queue that Timbers had taunted poor Stand-by by showing little bits of cheek. "You know how it is. Enough to make a boy think she hasn't got her drawers on. Oh yes she has. Then, oh no she hasn't." When Soapy heard that, he cackled close to choking. "It's as good as the old days!" But he didn't spoil the tale by saying that Emmie had seen none of it. The truth was, the cats in the alleys saw more than anyone. Sitting on bin lids, crouched under barrows or sneaking through holes in broken fences. But, like the stockily built matron, who spied from the back seat of a limousine parked on the crest of London Road, the cats said nothing.

"Five pounds used to buy twenty minutes with old Timberdick," Stand-by insisted. He had started to limp with an aching ankle and, every four or five steps, had to take little jumps to keep up.

"Bloody long time ago, that was. A dirty bloody fiver. God, it must be years since I pretended you were a big boy."

"Look Timbers, a fiver's worth twenty minutes," the police sergeant protested, "and we can walk through the runs and get to Tullet's Yard in twenty minutes."

Stand-by Moreton had always been too curious to be a good copper for Goodladies Road. Timbers couldn't be sure how much he had heard outside the phone box, so she needed to keep his mind on other things. She dodged about and stuck her hands in her coat pockets so that she could work her short raincoat to show off the best of her figure. The other girls had told her that Sergeant Moreton liked to see a bra, so she made sure that the coat's shoulders slipped and billowed enough to allow him a nice peep.[1] She was careful to keep herself out of reach, but not so far ahead that he would give up on her. It wasn't long before the sergeant was struggling to keep up so, when Timbers had put half a mile between them and Slowly's front door, she slowed to a dawdle.

"There's no need for this nonsense," he pleaded, holding his thigh and hobbling.

She leaned her shoulders against the slats of a fence. She bent one knee, pressed her heel on the wood and linked her hands behind her back. "I mean, when a measly fiver's all said and done," she sighed as he recovered his breath, "it won't say much about what you think of me." She looked this way and that, wondered if Stand-by had a cigarette, then she took on an expression that pretended she was waiting for something more interesting to happen.

"Look," Stand-by pressed his knuckles to his temples. "I don't want us to play around or anything. I said, look." How could he make her understand? "Look, I know other ways of doing this but this way's the nicest." He crossed the alley and sat on a dustbin.

"Oh, so it's information, is it? You want me to grass for a dirty bloody fiver. Mr Boniface used to give me three times that. Four times, sometimes. I told him about the thieving from the freight yard and Lillie Horsepool's moneylending in the docks. Do you think that he would have questioned May Tupner about her shady goings-on in St Mary's graveyard, if it had not been for me? Charlie

---

[1] Stand-by has never disclosed when he started his first sketchbook of brassieres. His wife insisted that it was not until their divorce, three years after the Naughty Wife Case, but that may have been a denial intended to reduce her embarrassment. By 1972, the leatherbound albums contained his drawings of three and a half thousand bras which he had observed on Goodladies Road. Some of the pictures were no more than a detail – a strap or lace trim. However, his expert evidence (and a carefully compiled index) convicted a tribe of sheep rustlers that year and probably saved the life of a young woman. Stand-by was well known to be a twerp, so his interest was regarded as eccentric rather than disreputable. I pushed the line that he had been working on a monograph in the style of Sherlock Holmes' study of cigar ash and bee stings.

Boniface and me, we used to meet on the path at the side of May's house. Sometimes, he'd be quite a father to me. That's if he wasn't feeling unsettled; then it was a different saucer of suet. Of course, I made up most of the stories. It was all fibs, mostly, but I think Mr Boniface knew that. He was happy for me to be nice to him, afters. Yes, whatever his mood, his afters kept him at attention. I made sure of that. What were you doing in those days, Stand-by? Worrying over some silly idea that would make you famous? 'The Stand-by Experiment' or 'Stand-by and the Pit', was it?"

Stand-by checked his watch. He hadn't paid her to waste time on some back alley slabs. They needed to move if they were going to reach Tullet's Yard before nine o'clock.

Timberdick pushed herself forward. She let her coat fall open, just enough to force naughty questions to the front of Stand-by's mind. It's here for the asking, she might have been saying. A boy's got to make a move, that's all.

When she saw no spark of interest, she raised the stakes. "How's your wife, Stand-by?" she asked, looking around, looking up at the sky, cocking her neck in case she had heard someone coming down a backyard path. She'd feel much better with a cigarette. "Does she still run half naked around the Elizabethan Rooms?"

"That's nothing to do with you!" he spat. "That happened last Christmas and it's all forgotten." He pushed himself off the bin and started to walk up and down. "I don't know what Ned's told you, but he exaggerates. Julie wasn't half naked."

"Well, I'll be buggered if she wasn't without a stitch. That's what I've heard."

"She was drunk!" he bawled.

"Yes, drunk. I've heard that as well. And disorderly with a whopping Welsh pony."

He shot across the path, grabbed her short hair and dragged her from the fence. She yelped and stamped. He caught her wrist in the air, turned it and twisted her arm up her back.

"You're hurting me, Stand-by!"

He spun her round, so that their eyes were like daggers drawn.

"Now look what you've done," he snarled, tightening his grip. "You've made me lose my temper and I never do that."

"So it's not grassing you're after. You really do want to bugger around with me, after all. Come on, Stand-by, we can do something for a fiver. I've never said that we can't."

He pulled her to the middle of the path, turned her so that they were both facing the same direction, then pushed her forward. "I'm not letting go, so walk nicely."

She knew that he wouldn't stop. She had always been able to spot the nasty little boy in class who answered teacher's questions sweetly, then did horrid things in secret.

"You're making me tip-toe, Stand-by. And I've lost my bloody sandal. You'll bloody pay for this. You little bastard."

"Shut up!" he snapped and pressed on her tortured arm.

"You're hurting!"

Back down the alley, the girl with the budgie had started to wail. Her mother and father were arguing and a neighbour was trying to clear up the mess.

"Don't go on about my Julie," Stand-by moaned, relaxing his grip. "She feels dreadful about it. She written sorry-letters to everyone. She's spoken to Ned on the phone, for an hour or more. Everything's settled, so don't go on about it."

That toddler on the trike, who had followed Timbers since early in the morning, pedalled excitedly along the paving slabs. Stand-by and Timbers leapt apart as he raced between them. He started to make the ee-or sounds of an ambulance.

* * *

Soapy laughed aloud as he told the story, much later. "I thought, he's gone and done it. He's nicked her, pinched her on the street." He had half a pint in front of him and the other gents had bought more in the tap. They loved it.

Len, the barman, loved it too. He made sure that the men could see the latest photo of Timberdick, pinned to the mahogany casing above the cash till. He'd already promised not to take it down unless Timbers marched in and complained. He nudged an open fag packet across the counter, egging Soapy on.

"I followed them as far as Tuppet's Yard, when they disappeared into the old warehouse. I heard Timbers scamper up the old wooden stairs and, seconds later, Stand-by came out and stood sentry on the pavement. I said to myself, 'Soapy, this ain't no ordinary arrest.' But I wouldn't have been worried if it hadn't been poor Stand-by. I couldn't trust him, could I? Who could, after all that his wife's been up to?"

"That's why they call him Stand-by," bellowed one of the others, holding his beer over his belly and already laughing at his own joke. "What are you doing in your wife's bed, Stand-by? We all know his answer. He's standing by in case she runs out of men!"

* * *

Timberdick had taken off her coat and was carrying her one surviving sandal. She was wearing her dress with buttons down the front but it was hardly enough. When the awkward, bony figure emerged from the trap door, the Chief Constable's wife pictured a waif in a bathing dress coming up from the millpond in their garden.

The top floor of Tullets was a nave of unpainted timbers with splinters and nailheads to catch a girl out. Great spars made Timbers look up to a lofty apex. The floor showed no scars from bearing crates or bails. No stores had been lodged against the uprights or manhandled through the trap. The place was so barren that even the birds sought somewhere else to nest. There were no windows but gaps in the eaves allowed some sunlight in and the sounds of the city drifted up from the street.

A solitary upturned orange box, at the far end of the hall, was the only furniture. The Chief Constable's wife stood behind it and didn't speak until Timbers had walked over the bare floorboards and was close enough to hear without the lady raising her voice.

"Stand-by and his wife have their own problems at the moment," she said. "Please excuse the sergeant's quick temper."

Timbers made much of her aching elbow. "He didn't ought to

have done it. Twisting me up like a chicken and marching me through the streets. I've got my standing to think of. My blokes don't expect to see me nicked like something common. I'm the top broad round here."

The lady smiled at the idea of this pint-sized tart laying down the law. "Broad?" She let the word weigh in the air. "How very 'Frank Sinatra'. Do you follow his films?"

"Some." Timbers bobbed on her feet, uncertain of what to say next. "I usually get into the Orient for nothing. The manager thinks very ..." But she didn't finish the sentence. She looked around and nibbled at her favourite thumbnail. " .. of me, see. What are we doing here?"

"You must be puzzled." The lady stepped forward from the orange box. "Allow me to introduce myself."

"You're Lady Brenda," said Timberdick, getting in first. "You're Rowena's mother and the Chief Constable's wife."

The lady dipped her head slightly as she smiled. "Although not in that order. I did manage to marry him first."

"Ned's not said much about you, but everyone knows you worked together on an important case once."

"1953," Lady Brenda conceded and went on smiling.

"And before that, during the war."

"We worked for different departments in those days. It often felt that we were on different sides. Ned has a reputation for being lazy, these days."

"He's a fat slob," said Timbers, expecting ready agreement.

"But he has done some brave things for his country. He deserves an easy twilight to his working life. It all seems a long time ago. I am largely retired now. They wheel me out to interview army-types or reassure public servants with faint hearts. You could say that I work a little from home."

"Oh," said Timbers,"so we do have something in common."

"You wouldn't like me, Timberdick. You'd call me one of those scary old partridges who sit on committees, break champagne bottles over racing yachts and visit schools where I tell young ladies what not to do. But any honest fellow will say that my life's not as frothy or self-important as that. I keep an eye on people who have helped me in the past. In this instance, Ned and yourself."

"I've never helped you," Timbers declared.

"Oh but you have, my darling." She exaggerated her smile but didn't explain. From the moment that Lady Brenda called her darling, Timberdick realised that the lady was right; Timbers didn't like the woman.

"Timberdick, I've brought you here because I have worrying news. Connie Freya has broken out of prison."

Timbers held back a laugh. "How come? The last I heard, she was muddle-headed and always in tears. Even if she climbed over the fence, she wouldn't know the way home."

"She was employed on the prison farm and wandered off. I agree, if it hadn't been so simple, she might not have managed it."

"Well, it was nothing to do with me. I've not seen her round here."

"She burned down The Hoboken Arms last night and murdered Constable Dickin. We believe that she has also killed her old Navy commander. He hasn't been seen since the fire but we've yet to find his body. It was the gentleman's disappearance that prompted the duty officer to call me in the middle of the night. The dead Admiral is a body which we'd rather not misplace. I realised how serious the situation was as soon as I heard about the arson and Connie Freya's escape. You may find a number of us observing Goodladies Road over the next few days. We don't want matters to get out of hand. Ned is safely under guard."

"Who's with him? Please don't tell me it's those two WRAC tarts."

"What do you know about Alice and Bernice?" asked Lady Brenda.

"Nothing. But Ned won't cope with two women looking after him. You know what that'll do to him."

"Did you see the girls in The Hoboken Arms before the fire?"

Timberdick shook her head "I was there from nine o'clock. They weren't downstairs in the bar."

"Afterwards? Alice was seen in the yard, shortly before Archie's body was found. Did you see her there?"

"I wouldn't have," Timbers explained. "I didn't go into the yard. I watched from the pavement, then I went back to Ma's place. I thought Ned was going to spend the night with us."

"Well, Ned is safe enough, but what about you, Timberdick? The Freya woman knows that you solved the murder of Yvonne Young. You sent her to prison."

"Don't worry about me."

Timbers looked at the haughty face and tried to understand what made the woman untouchable. She had an all-knowing look about her. She knew everything about Timberdick, not just her history but her nature too. She even knew what Timbers was likely to do next. Her eyes had a terseness. Yes, and it was in her mouth and the set of her cheeks. Nothing could surprise her. She had seen it all before.

But it was more than all these things.

She had authority, that same savvy that had prompted spiteful competitors to call her Lady Brenda years before she took the title. She knew the ways that things got done. She had the right phone numbers and the right people were watching out for her. Everything was there, for her to call on. Nothing could touch her.

"My information is that you and your baby are living with Martha Shipley," she was saying. "Perhaps that's no longer true?"

"Things got difficult when Ma's daughter was released. Baz can be very jealous. We all agreed that Ma would carry on looking after my young 'un and I would keep clear for a few months."

"So where are you sleeping?"

Timbers shrugged. "Nowhere." Then, looking around: "Not here. That's for certain. It's bloody freezing."

"The wind gets under the eaves."

Timberdick pouted. "Everything's fine. I want my Little Timbs to be with Ma Shipley. That's what's important. She'll be a better mother than me, although she gets cross when I say it. She calls herself 'Nanny' and that's fine too. I don't want any noses poking in."She started to walk away, down the long stretch of bare floorboards, the dirty dust sticking to her soles.

"What about Glenn Miller?"

Timbers turned at the door. "You think Glenn Miller's got something to do with my baby? You're crackers. Let me tell you: my Little Timbs' grandad is a dead Superintendent."

"I know that. But Yvonne Young often said that she had seen Glenn Miller in Paris when he was supposed to be dead. Then she was murdered by Connie Freya. Now, Connie Freya has escaped from prison and people are saying that the Twinwood Trombone is on The Goodladies Road." She explained, "Twinwood was Glenn Miller's last airfield."

Timbers kept a satisfied snigger to herself. Only strangers put 'the' in front of Goodladies, so Lady Brenda wasn't as well-in as she pretended. Timbers retraced her steps and perched uncomfortably on the corner of the orange box. "Listen, Chiefie. I know what Twinwood is. I can tell you everything about Glenn Miller. Go on, ask me any question."

But Lady Brenda was a good inquisitor and she knew when to keep her powder dry. She put her head down, just a little, and waited for Timbers to use up all those stories that could help her avoid giving away too much information. No-one spoke. It became a competition.

They heard Stand-by Moreton idly kicking a pebble against the kerbstones. He tried to whistle but he couldn't hold a tune and soon gave up. For a moment, a funny comment about him seemed to hover on Lady Brenda's lips, but she kept quiet.

Timberdick broke the silence. "Look, I sat through the film twice and didn't take my eyes off the screen. I studied it like no other person in the picture-house. A weirdo had paid to go in with me. Then he says that he wants to do me in the middle of everyone else. I told him, there's a house for doing that in, down by the railway lines. I mean, I wasn't about to upset the manager of the Orient, was I? But I did take his money, why not? And I made sure that I kept my eyes dead straight, learning every line from the picture, twice over. So I know all about Glenn Miller."

"Where is the Twinwood Trombone?"

"How would I know?" Timbers exclaimed.

"It went missing after the carol concert. Archie was sure that Alice and Bernice had stolen it, so he followed them to The Hoboken Arms. But, if they had it, they got rid of it before the fire. So where is it, Timberdick?"

"I don't know."

The two clever women stared at each other, a game of she knows that I know, and she knows that I know she knows that I know.

Timberdick squared up to the woman's face. "Alright. You're in charge. You've been in charge for so long that people do what you say without thinking. Important people listen to what you say. Everyone runs up to you with information and ideas. That puts you in the middle of things and, bugger me, how you like it! But I'm just as brainy as you, and one day I'll show you. Don't think you'll ever get the better of me because, when it comes to winning between you and me, I'll never come second."

"Why, my dear girl."

Timberdick stamped her foot. "Dont – dear girl me!" She stepped back from the orange box. "I tell you our Yvonne never saw or heard Glenn-bloody-Miller. She wasn't born then and she'd never been to Paris."

"She could have seen him, if Mr Miller's still alive," argued Lady Brenda. "And who said he stayed in France?"

Timbers was walking away again. "You've had too much bed with your husband, Chiefie. You've caught 'policeman's brain' They all suffer from it. They get an idea in their heads and, whatever they see or hear, gets stretched or shaved to fit in place. Glenn Miller, still alive and living in England? Rubbish! But believe what you like. Most people do and they die happy." Without turning, she waved a hand in the air.

She was at the door before Lady Brenda called to her: "Timberdick! Women call WRNS officers 'Chiefie'. I rather like it."

* * *

Weeks later, when Christmas was over and Archie Dickin's killer was due for trial, the landlord of The Volunteer would invite a small group of his regulars to join him before opening time. It was, by then, well known that events early in the morning of December 16 would be an important part of the prosecution's evidence and locals wanted to hear Soapy Berkeley's version before it came out in court.

"Mighty things are wrong here, I thought, and it's up to Soapy Berkeley to find them out."

"Good old Soapy, on the trail of a murderer!"

"I didn't know it was murder then, did I?" Soapy insisted irritably. "You lot are wise after the event, when the murderer's been caught and the corpse has been buried. But then, on the day – on the day, that's what I'm talking about – I just had it in my bones that matters were odd."

By the time Soapy Berkeley was ready to describe Timberdick's exit from the warehouse, his audience had ordered more drinks and someone had passed a packet of Hamlets around. Soapy was sitting on a bar stool, the soiled hem of his winter coat brushing the floor, his cold fingers shivering as he held a smouldering cigar in one hand and a whiskey in the other. A portly chap in braces stood at his shoulder, close enough to nudge Soapy's ribs. There was a lean, drop-shouldered Midlander who spoke through his ale. He had a toothbrush moustache and hair over his ears (did he think he was a Beatle?) His suit was too big and he made it worse by keeping the middle button of his jacket done up. You're no better than I am, thought Soapy.

Worst of all, Emmie Dawson had turned up and, although she stayed at her table, drinking her stout, her presence took the gloss off Soapy's opportunity. Miss Dawson knew almost as much as he did, but Soapy so rarely had the chance to take centre stage that he resolved to make the most of it.

He reminded them of the background. "Before six o'clock that morning, Timbers had been running through Goodladies Junction on her way to Slowly Barnes' diggings. Urgent business, that's what it looked like, but she was there for less than twenty minutes before she was out and whispering in the telephone box. A frantic call, I remarked at the time. But she doesn't go back to Slowly's place. No, she's very happy to get herself arrested and marched off to Tullet's. Why not the police station? Even when she comes out of the warehouse, she doesn't go back to Slowly. So, I thought, Soapy's got to find out what's amiss at that particular address."

"Aye, and we all know what you found," said the man in braces.

"You do know it now, days and days later, because you've read it all in the papers. But nobody knew anything then. It was just the unhappiness in Soapy's stomach, that's all. I hurried back to Slowly's house and, when I got there, I saw a horse ambulance with R.N. markings on the sides."

"No, you didn't. The Navy's got no horses."

"They have," argued the man with the middle button done up. "How else would they manoeuvre field guns over rocky terrain? The Crimea, Gallipolli."

"Maybe they've got no horses," conceded Soapy. "But they've got horse ambulances because I saw one outside Slowly Barnes' home, and two men were loading a large wooden box into it."

"A box! A coffin's more likely!"

"But I didn't know what it was at the time. It could have been stolen gold for all I knew."

Len, the landlord, leaned over the bar. "So you went inside, did you Soapy?"

"And Slowly was nowhere to be seen. Vanished, she had. All that I found was the golden trumpet."

"You mean, trombone," piped up Emily Dawson.

Soapy responded grudgingly. "Yes, trombone."

"I don't think you went into the house at all," she accused, dribbling her stout.

"What would you know about that?"

"I know more than anybody, don't I? Wasn't Emily Dawson the one who gave Timberdick the final clue to the mystery. Without Emily Dawson, she wouldn't have caught the killer. You all know that, don't you?"

But they took no notice because this was a blokes' party.

"If you went inside, you were the last person to see it," suggested Len, "until Timbers turned up with it for the trial."

"I'd say I was," Soapy agreed, careful not to make too much of the story.

"And Slowly's flat was unlocked?" Emily challenged from the back.

"Of course. Otherwise, how did I get in?"

"And you left the trombone just where you found it." She was on her feet now and slopping the drink from her glass.

"Of course I did. I wasn't going to steal it, was I?"

"A good job you didn't," guffawed the portly one and raised his tankard at the picture of Timberdick above the till.

SEVEN

The Fighting Naughty Wife

While Timberdick was running from Tullet's warehouse, the record dealer was setting out his stall, half a mile away. Other traders were still manoeuvring their vans and trucks over the cobbles. With only two Thursdays before Christmas, Sean wanted to attract those early shoppers who trudged through the street-market on their way to work. His transistor radio, strapped to the scaffolding that would separate him from Rita's stall of rejected shoes, predicted rain after lunch so he was determined to push his best offers early on. There would be no Beatles single for Christmas this year and their December album was only a collection of oldies. Sean had cut an advert from the Melody Maker and sellotaped it to the peg-board at the back. He had no copies to sell (Sean's stock was secondhand, or new but in damaged sleeves, or new but dodgy) but Beatle fans were hawk-eyed and he knew they wouldn't miss the box of bootlegs beneath the poster.

He rubbed his cold hands together and looked up and down the market for the teenage girl who had been gone for twenty minutes. She was half way up the aisle, handing white paper bags of toasted sandwiches to the dealers. By the time she delivered Sean's bacon with brown sauce, the breakfast snack would be cold. If he mentioned it, she would scrape a refund from her tips. Then he would pour hot tea from his Thermos into two plastic beakers and, if he was lucky again, she would make his stall her base throughout the day. Having Molly on hand allowed him to get amongst the other stallholders in search of bargains.

But Molly was caught in conversation at the cotton and thread stand. Sean stuck his hands in the cash apron around his waist, turned his back to the stall and buried himself in a box of records.

A familiar, shrill voice yapped: "It's going to pour down this afters."

He straightened up to find Timberdick's poky face peering over the counter.

"Your knees look frozen," he said.

"They're bloody red, aren't they? They're perished. Bloody Stand-by just nicked me and kept me in Tullet's warehouse for half an hour. Bloody liberty. I've run all the way from there to here. Aren't you going to let me round the back and find a rug for my legs?"

"What do you want, Timbers?"

Sean pushed the box of Sinatra's Christmas 78s to the front of the stall. Last year, Mark from the model shop had been interested in them. This year, Sean hoped the old man would give way to the temptation.

Timberdick had already settled herself in his deck chair and was sorting through the bundle of blankets and curtains. "These are all filthy," she complained.

"They've been on the milk float. They're for covering up crates of records." He stood over her, trying to make her feel in the way. "What do you want?"

"Do you want me to go for a couple of sarnies?"

"I've already got a bacon and brown sauce coming."

"Well, give me three and six and I'll get two fresh ones from the caravan," she said. "I'll screw him for two coffees at the same time."

"What do you want, Timberdick?"

"Just saying hello, aren't I? I told you, I've run all the way from Tullet's warehouse." She leaned forward in the deck chair and looked up and down the street. Plainly, she wasn't going to move until she was ready. "Shout if you see the Number Four turn up The Avenue. I want to catch it on the way back. I'm going to take a look at Ned's place."

"Have you chosen his Christmas present yet?" He reached for

an LP which he had put to one side. "Here, put this one in his stocking."

"If he's getting stockings, he's getting me in them." She looked at the record sleeve. "Is it Red Nichols?"

"It's says Glenn Miller, doesn't it?"

"It's Red Nichols he likes, or the Squadronaires. Have you got any Squadronaires?"

"He was looking at that one, last week. Glenn Miller."

She tapped her head with a knuckle as if she really was trying to work something out. "What goes on round here? Everyone wants to talk about Glenn Miller. Are we all working up to a Glenn Miller Christmas on Goodladies Road?"

"Something like that. The Hoboken Arms' old jazz band has asked me to put a Christmas show on the pirate radio, with them playing Glenn Miller music."

Timbers was in no hurry to progress the conversation. She knew that her time-wasting was irritating the record man and she meant to enjoy it. She didn't look up as she read the listing on the album sleeve. "I thought you'd been busted?"

"Warned off, that's all. I've kept my head down since the summer so two hours on Christmas Day won't harm. Are you going to buy that one?"

"Do you remember that story you told me about Glenn Miller in Paris, after he was dead?"

"Yes. He was seen in a brothel in 1947. The old bugger in the Curiosity Shop saw him. Of course, he's dead now – the old bugger, I mean – so you can't ask him. His wife's gone too. Mind, they've not cleared their junk shop yet. I keep thinking about that."

"It wasn't him that told you. He was never in France. You're talking about his sister Els."

"Maybe. She was there. But the old bugger told me about it."

"Maybe," Timbers agreed. "Maybe it was Els who brought the trombone back."

"Oh, don't start on about the wretched trombone. I've had enough of it. I had a bloke round the stall yesterday, going over and over it. For two hours, he stood here and he didn't buy a thing." He dipped his hand into his money pockets and brought out three and six. "Here, go for a pack of two sandwiches."

"He didn't want this record then?"

"No. He didn't want any record. He just wanted to know who the Glenn Miller enthusiasts were on Goodladies Road. Two sandwiches, Timbers."

"I'm comfy now. I've only just got my knees warm."

"But you said."

"Can't Molly fetch them for you?"

"She's supposed to be coming."

"So you won't need two more from me, will you?"

He asked again, "Are you going to buy that record for Ned?"

"What did you tell this strange man?"

"I told him to talk with Ned Machray and the band at The Hoboken Arms."

"And the old Curisoity Shop? Surely you told him about that?"

"Yes, I think I did." Sean looked at the sky and held out a palm, checking for rain. "You know, he looked just like Buddy Holly."

Timberdick almost missed the Number Four. When she saw the bus pull up, she waved her hand and shouted, but the street was full of Christmas shoppers and they all seemed to be rushing in the wrong direction. She stumbled over a dog-lead and went sideways when an old woman barged her, but she managed to reach the bus stop as the conductor was ringing the bell. Then, at the last second, another woman jumped off, shouted "Oh!" and skipped back on, tripping Timbers to her knees. The conductor reached out, grabbed her puny arm and hauled her on baord.

"You're not to cause trouble," he warned as Timbers recovered herself on the platform. "I've heard about last Friday. Playing Jessie up like you did. Any more of that here and I'll throw you off. Where do you think you're going, my lady? Not upstairs, you're not. You're sitting down here where I can keep an eye on you."

"I've got no money."

"Then you can walk from the next stop."

"Can't we talk about it when you're out late one night?"

"Go and sit down, Timberdick. The rules are: you don't talk, you don't move and you don't stare." He put her in a seat half way down the aisle.

An old dear with a dog on her lap said, "How do you do, Timberdick?" with extra politeness and licked her lips.

"Very nicely, Mrs. P."

The young wife who had jumped in front of Timbers was already arranging herself in the seat ahead. She leaned back and said, "I've been looking for you. That's why I got off at the market. Then I saw you get on, so I did too. Again, I mean. Got on again. Got back on." She started afresh, "I saw you get on so I jumped back on. After you. After I saw you."

The bus was climbing the steep hill through a housing estate. Each change to a lower gear made the passengers wonder if the vehicle would stall and never get going again. They started to hold on, the more nervous pressed their toes to the floor. It was a relief that no-one was waiting at the next stop. The engine seemed to shudder sideways, making the body of the bus rock on its axles.

"Miss Woodcock," the young woman shouted over the motor. "I want to say how sorry Sergeant Moreton is."

"You're his wife?"

Mrs P leaned forward and whispered loudly, "She is. She's Mrs Stand-by. Stand-by's wife."

The woman nodded. "I am." She opened her handbag and dipped her fingers inside. "Would you like me to pay your fare?"

Mrs P interrupted again. "Do that and him with the tickets will be disappointed. He likes Timberdick to owe him things."

"Don't call me Woodcock, either," said Timbers. "You know my name round here. The last time a woman called me Woodcock, she stuck me in remand for seven days."

"Miss Timberdick then. My husband didn't mean to grab you this morning. This year has left him very mixed up."

"You saw him do it?" Timbers asked.

"Sounds like she did," mouthed old Mrs P, nodding excitedly to attract Timbers' attention. The dog looked upwards for a kiss but she pushed his nose down again.

"I hope you won't take the matter any further. He doesn't need a complaint on top of everything else."

"Don't worry about that. I'll just get my own back."

Mrs P nodded wisely.

"Really, he's had enough trouble," said the sergeant's wife. "Most of it brought on by me, I'm afraid. Entirely unjustified, mind."

"What were you doing in the alley before seven this morning?" asked Timbers.

"I wanted to catch him up. I wanted to explain about last night."

"Well, now. My Pontefract man always said, if you can't find the guts to confess beforehand, then you've got no strength to stand the storm after."

"Oh, but no," protested Mrs Stand-by. "You've misunderstood."

"My Pontefract man was full of little bits of wisdom. He's dead now. Died in prayer, I've heard. He always did a lot of praying."

"But you've got it wrong. I don't need to admit anything about another man. I've never been unfaithful to my husband and I don't mean to be."

"That's not what I've heard," Timbers said quickly, recalling tales from the dinner dance.

"Oooh," said Mrs P, bending towards the sergeant's wife. "Did you hear that, lovey? Ooh, no, no. I don't think you should allow that."

The woman looked for Timbers' reaction. "Oh, I'm sure she was just being cheeky."

"Oooh, no, lovey. No, I don't think cheeky at all. Timbers, you weren't being cheeky, were you?"

Timbers looked away, cocksure, as she said, "I was thinking of the Polaroids from the police ball with this lady, piggy bare, being chased by a Welsh sailor."

"You bitch!" shouted the slandered wife. She was on her feet, the conductor was already marching up the aisle, and Mrs P made the most of the opportunity.

"Go on, lovey," she shouted. "Stand up for youself. Stand up for Stand-by!"

"Yeah?" Timbers taunted. "Stand up for him, if you can. You flighty old cow."

"How dare you! How dare you say such horrid things. About me! Me, about me! Just look at yourself, you dirty tart!"

Timbers jumped up, but had to hold on because the bus went too fast round a corner. "What did you say?"

"Dirty tart!"

"What!"

"Dirty tart!" said Mrs Stand-by, ready to say it again.

"Go on! Go on! Say it again!"

"Dirty tart!"

"Again!" shouted Timberdick. Both hands were on her hips now. Her little bottom was pressed against the chrome frame of a seat. Her feet were spread apart, keeping her steady.

"Dirty tart!" sang Mrs Stand-by. "Dirty tart. Dirty tart. Dirty tart!"

"Oh yeah?" Timbers shouted as she moved into the middle of the aisle.

Their eyes locked; there was just the hint of a nod – a 'yes' – then the girls went for each other's hair, screaming and stamping as they tumbled to the floor. The conductor rushed to get between them, but Mrs P blocked his way. "Fight-fight-fight!" chanted the little old lady and, if her arms hadn't been full of puppy dog, she would have clapped her hands.

"I'm not a dirty tart like you!" the wife wailed from the floor, with Timbers on top. She punched and kicked with no idea where the blows might land.

"I bite!" squeaked Timbers, half teasing.

"No!" Mrs Stand-by shrieked, hitting wildly.

Timberdick joined in, thrashing about and squealing excitedly.

The dog jumped from the old woman's arms and scampered around the kicking feet of the wrestlers.

"Off! Off my bus!" But every time that the conductor tried to grab an arm or a leg, the dog got in the way, and he stumbled into an empty seat. "Off! You two! Off!" He stood on the seat and rang the bell repeatedly.

"Off! Off!" Mrs P took up the chant, more often heard at the strip shows around Goodaldies Junction. "Off-off-off!"

The driver pulled up at the kerb, and switched on the alarm horn in his cab.

"Oooh! They're in trouble now," drooled Mrs P. "Come on, Tiggy. See them off."

The pup started to snap at the girls' feet, chasing them to the platform at the back of the bus. Timbers put one arm around the woman, so that one or the other wouldn't fall over, and Mrs Stand-by pressed a hand against Timbers' tummy.

"Filthy women!" shouted Mrs P. "Throw them off!"

The shout brought even greater effort from the terrier. His jaws got so close to their ankles that the girls were eager to jump off as soon as they could.

They both fell onto the pavement. Three or four youths gathered round as the women tried to straighten their clothes, then they went off laughing and calling out.

"Disgraceful" said a grandmother with a pushchair. "Disgraceful behaviour."

"Mrs P called us filthy women?" queried the policeman's wife.

"That was your fault. Showing everything you've got. Skirt up and legs in the air. You're a show-off, Jools."

The woman smiled at the use of a pet name. "I have never been thrown of a bus before," she said, dabbing a graze on her knee. "It tickles, doesn't it? Please don't tell my Tommy."

"Tommy?"

"Sergeant Moreton."

"Oh yes, I see. I've only ever heard people call him Stand-by," Timbers said.

Mrs Stand-by perked up. "Do you know why people call him that? I only found out the other day. You see, as a young recruit he had studied his radio procedure classes so diligently that he began to use the same words over the telephone. He finished each phone call with 'Standing by'. Actually, I don't think he's used the words for years." Then she realised that Timbers wasn't paying attention. "It's not very interesting, is it?"

No, not interesting at all, thought Timbers. "What were you going to tell him about last night?"

"Do I sound like a policeman's wife?"

"Only every bit of you," Timbers answered.

"I still don't know if I should tell Tommy what I saw. On the one hand, it's the right thing to do. On the other, it would be too much for him. Ah, but it's still bound to come out." She shrugged. "I really don't know if I should."

They had been deposited at the top of the hill, and a mammoth housing estate, stretched out below them, promised a long walk home. "That'll take till Christmas," whined Mrs Stand-by. "Let's sit on the pavement for a bit."

"You saw the murder, didn't you?"

"Yes. No, not exactly. I saw the shadows of the murder. I had been walking up and down Goodladies Road, looking for PC Dickin. He'd been telling stories about me and I wanted him to stop. I saw his wife. I saw you, showing yourself at the junction. Very leggy, you were too." Mrs Stand-by waited, but Timberdick didn't object. "And I saw the heavy woman, looking like an old fashioned midwife. But most of all, I saw PC Dickin's wife. So I followed her. I thought, where the wife is, the husband must be nearby. But he wasn't."

A breeze caught them and she pulled her clothes close. Beyond the housing estate, they could see the ribbon of dual carriageways, then the town centre flats, warehouse yards and old fashioned chimneys, and, beyond that, the busy harbour. "It is nice, up here," remarked Stand-by's wife, "watching everyone being busy down there."

Timberdick said, "Pity there's not a chip shop," and waited for the woman to continue her story.

"Mrs Dickin walked to the bottom of Goodladies Road but she didn't meet Archie. No. Rather! Rather a young man with glasses and black hair. Long and stringy."

"Like Hank Marvin from The Shadows?"

"Ah, Hank B Marvin. I remember seeing him on stage in 1959. Mind, I was a married woman by then so I couldn't act too much like a lovesick teenager, but I was in the third row and he was up on the stage and, ah, he looked lovely." She sighed, "We had an eye to eye moment." She shook the picture from her mind. "I went with Mavis Rhodes from across the way. She arranged it all and we pretended that I only went because she wanted me to. I couldn't let my Tommy know what I was always thinking about Hank B Marvin, so I said I preferred Cliff. But that was nonsense. Oooh, I used to think about him most nights, after that concert. You know what it can do to a girl. You've felt it, Timberdick. Ah, when I think of it now...." Then her daydreams fractured. "No, this man was nothing like Hank B Marvin. More like Buddy Holly."

"You followed them to The Hoboken Arms?" Timbers asked.

The woman put her thoughts in order, then reported, "I saw the police car stop outside the pub so I hurried back up the road. Ned went inside first, leaving Archie in the car. I thought, here's my chance to have it out with him, but Mrs Dickin got in the way. She pulled the car door open and they started to argue. I stayed clear and followed Ned into the Hoboken."

"Why?"

"It's not important."

Timberdick insisted. "Why did you follow Ned?"

"Because Stand-by's in trouble and I wanted to ask Ned for help. He's always been a good friend to Stand-by. But I found out that he was shut in a room with two women. I went up and listened at the door. I realised that he wouldn't be coming out soon, so I walked away. I got to the top of the stairs and saw that the kitchen was on fire. Of course, I didn't know how serious it was. When I looked out of the landing window, the flames were lighting up the backyard. I saw shapes against the wall. A man was on his knees and he was being beaten with a stick or an iron bar."

"Did you hear anything?"

"I heard it was a woman doing it."

EIGHT

Sergeant Timberdick!

The Farlington Freight, no taller than a mouse's back, crept so slowly from the chalk cliff tunnel that the plastic figures beside the speedway track seemed hardly to notice. If this 12.20 light goods train reached Tottering before the Express, it would be held at signals. In turn, the Seaside Special from Waterloo wouldn't get through.

Betty 'Slowly' Barnes, crouching down so that her gleeful eyes were level with trees made from old toilet brushes, knew that she had to get her timing right. Otherwise, it would take her twenty minutes to bring the railway back on schedule. If she could remember the correct sequence, that is. She knew that the layout was a fictional representation of two Hampshire junctions which made it reasonable for old stock from different companies to appear, but wasn't there a rule of 'pre-grouping embargo'? Well, never mind that. She was running trains that I had already assembled so she supposed that the make-ups were correct. With growing confidence, she pressed on. She brought the Seaside Special within two curves of Tottering Little Junction and withdrew the News of the World train to the fiddle yard. She opened the points at the far end of the room, bringing the deep red Midlander (eight coaches, all corridor) into play. She tucked her bottom lip behind the top row of front teeth and gave the scene one last check as the Express cleared the (newly constructed) viaduct and straightened out for the downhill run. The truth was, Betty had already heard the back door open and wanted four trains up and running before Timberdick reached the second floor of Shooter's Grove.

Slowly had been alone in the rambling Victorian house for ninety minutes. The sign in the front garden said that it was a Divisional Training School for policemen, but it had been years since anyone sat in the classrooms. My lodgings were on the top floor but, slowly and surely, I had made myself the warden of the place. My Police Dance Orchestra rehearsed twice a week on the ground floor, where two rooms stored their junk. I had an office on the first floor and the beginnings of a museum in three back rooms. (No-one knew about that yet.) My model railway ran between a classroom and a dormitory on the second floor.

For twelve months, Betty 'Slowly' Barnes had visited Shooter's Grove every Monday morning, when we played trains together for two hours at a time. She was a natural, and when she planned to surprise Timberdick with an express train, she did it perfectly. The sleek Silver Link, with twelve coaches in tow, gathered speed as it rounded the curve at the bedroom door and it was racing along the landing as Timberdick reached the top of the stairs. With laudable restraint, Slowly didn't release the whistle which I had rigged to the bedroom ceiling.

"What's going on!" demanded Timbers, her hands on her hips, her feet apart. "You're supposed to be hiding."

"I am. Oh, I tried to stay shut in Ned's old boot room but it made me think too much. I had too many pictures in my head, Timbs. So I came up here. No-one's seen me."

"Never mind his bloody boot room. You're not supposed to be here. Stay put, I said. Stay in your bed while I got things sorted. Hell, I can't believe this. Two hours ago you were scared of being hung. Now, you're playing with toy bloody trains. Woman, this is a serious mess we're in!"

The girls were standing at the bannister post, their feet either side of a used pair of socks and underpants that I had dropped there, two days ago.

"I couldn't stay at my place, Timbers. I just couldn't. Not even when they'd taken his body away, I couldn't, knowing that he'd been there and what he looked like, red and bruised and all the wrong bits bloating. I had to run away."

Timberdick looked at the state of her old friend. They had worked the pavements of Goodladies Road for twenty years. They didn't really like each other but it was difficult to avoid being friends after all that time. When Timberdick and Slowly spoke of all the girls they had known, they realised that they were the only ones who had started when the war was over and still worked on Goodladies Road.

Betty Barnes was five feet tall and much too wide. Her blouse was buttoned up wrong and she had tucked the waistband of her skirt higher on one side, so that the hem of ribbed knitting stopped five inches above one knee and seven inches above the other. Her shoes had stretched where she had walked on the sides. Everything was too tight so that everything else, not just her clothes, was stretched out of shape. Her thighs were fat and kissed all the way down. Her arms were fat: Timbers expected them to squeak at the tops even when they didn't. Her face was fat, so that her eyes and her pinched mouth sat in little pies of podgy flesh. Her nose was like an on-off switch that Ned Machray always wanted to tweak.

"I could hear you playing trains, Slo'. I was walking up the front garden path and I could hear you, plain as day."

"No-one's seen me," Slowly repeated. "You don't understand. Model railways are good for me. They calm me down. Everything's in order. I know what's going to happen. I've as much control as I want, and if I don't want any, I can sit back and watch. I can set up a world and it never goes wrong. Ned and I, we've shared some lovely times in here. For hours, every Monday morning. It's lasted almost a year, in spite of you saying that we couldn't do it anymore."

Timbers took her friend's hand, leading her away from the landing window. "Ned won't be coming back, Slo'. Not for some time. Something's happened."

"Did you know that he spent all night with the dead man's wife," Slowly blurted. "The mad-woman next-to-hers caught me when I was running from my place to here, and she said he went in at midnight and didn't come out again."

"He'd be in a state," Timberdick argued. "What with the fire and saving lives. She'd have told him to sleep over, Slo'. Of course, she would. But that doesn't mean anything. You're not saying that it does, are you? They won't have done anything together. God, Slowly, Ned would never have taken advantage of her, like that. I mean, God, the bloke had been dead less than a couple of hours. Besides, Ned'd be in no state."

"I'm only saying."

"What do you mean, mad-woman?"

"The one with one good arm and one bad one. He must have told you about her. They were nearly in love before the war. This ..." Slowly pretended to click two fingers in the air, but couldn't. "This, you know, fortune-type-of-woman promised that they were going to get married later in life. Really, Timbs, hasn't he told you? Surely? He told me all about it one Monday morning. The electrics were off so we couldn't play trains."

"Alright, Slowly. I'm sure that I don't have to know."

"We did a pot of milky coffee on the gas and took it out to the back garden. I remember the sun was shining and it was really hot. Really, really hot. Oh, it was ever so nice. He was telling me all about it, but lazily, and thinking in between the bits. It was one of those moments, with Ned, when you think you really know him. You feel so close to him. You've had them, too?"

"Slowly, I said there's no need."

"I remember little flakes of blossom falling from the trees, and the sounds of bees and butterflies,"

"I said, alright! Shut up!"

Slowly said nothing.

She allowed Timberdick a few moments to calm down, then asked, "Who told you Ned's not coming back?"

"The Chief Constable's wife. Something's happened, Slo'. Connie Freya's escaped from prison."

Slowly laughed. "What with? A tin opener?"

"They think that she set fire to the Hoboken and killed Archie Dickin. They've even got her name down for your dead Admiral."

"Well, don't let's tell them not," said Slowly.

"Ned's life is in danger."

"That won't keep him away beyond Tuesday," said Slowly. "The DeLuxe Electric Signal Set is due in the shops. Mark can only get six boxes so Ned will want to be sure of his."

Timberdick shook her head. "For God's Sake, trains aren't the most important thing in his life!"

The podgy woman considered the point. She thought, sometimes trains are the most important and sometimes I'm the most important. But she didn't say anything. At least, she never came second to jazz music.

Without warning, Slowly shouted a shrill 'Hello!' that rang around the old building. "I love this house," she laughed, her hands pressed to her groin. "It's smashing!" The childish exclamation was so typical of her. At work, Slowly was more vulgar and strident than any of the girls but, in her own time, she went back to the days when her life was straightforward and she found fun in simple things. She enjoyed the jokes that she had enjoyed at school. "Have you ever been in Shooter's Grove on your own?" she asked. "It's a scream. I run up and down the staircases, into the old classrooms, shouting my head off. No wonder Ned loves living here. Fancy having two staircases, Timbs. Two staircases!" She burst into laughter. "One for up and one for down!"

Timbers responded soberly. "You've spent too much bloody time here, Slowly Barnes."

"Timbs, let's turn all the taps on! All the taps in the house. I bet there's twenty!"

But Timbers chose not to join in. She listened to Slowly's squeals and delighted shrieks as she ran from floor to floor, letting the water spill into the washbasins and baths. The water pressure was high in Shooter's Grove; the taps released gushes of water, some of it scalding hot. But Timbers couldn't bring herself to take part in the prank. When Slowly had run out of steam, and her laughter reduced to breathy panting, Timbers stepped into the second floor bathroom, announced that she was going to soak for half an hour, and closed the door behind her.

The bath was already half full, thanks to Slowly's enthusiasm, and much too hot to get into. She topped it up, letting the cold tap run as she undressed, and she was easing herself into the water when Slowly called, "Where are you, Timbs? What are you up to?"

Timberdick didn't answer. She closed her eyes and sank deliciously deeper beneath the surface. She felt the water on her cheeks and chin .

"Timberdick. You can't hide from me. I shall find you."

Then the door opened. Slowly tossed a couple of bath towels into the room. "Wait there. I'll come back." And when she did, she was carrying a sketch pad and crayons under her arm. She settled herself on the edge of the bath and told Timberdick to keep still. "Don't smile, though. It's not about smiling."

"I didn't know you could draw, Slo'"

"Neither did I until I found loads and loads of drawing paper in one of the old classrooms. I started with trains. Then, I did Ned. Do you want to see the ones I've done of Ned? I can run and get them for you. But I've been wanting to do you for ages." She worked quickly, but it wasn't all good. She tried to rub bits out and, twice, she tore a sheet from the pad and started again. So, Miss Slowly Barnes not only visited Shooter's Grove each Monday, but her feet were sufficiently under the table for her to keep her drawings here. Probably, she had her own drawer or cupboard. Because Timberdick wanted to know how Slowly would draw her, she played the game and kept still, but she felt the tips of her ears turn pink and, for the first time, she recognised that the knots in her tummy were jealousy.

"I don't want you to talk about you and Ned spending time together," she said.

"I only do it to rub it in," said Slowly without looking up. The crayon raced over the paper.

"It's horrid when you do." Timbers sighed, "I think I'm losing him, Slo', and it hurts like buggery. A couple of years ago, he was always asking to marry me and I said no, over and over. Now, maybe we will never get married. I don't think we've ever been lovers in the proper sense. But it's worse than all that. I'm losing him as a friend. I don't think he cares. He doesn't even think of me, most of the time."

Slowly drew quickly on the pad, her mouth moved in circles like a child's in concentration. Throughout that autumn, I had spoken to her about my feelings for Timberdick, and this moment in the bathroom may have been a good time for her to give away some clues. As she tried to put the right words together, she allowed other thoughts to the front of her mind. "Just think what Archie was shouting when he was murdered. 'I'm only here to get my trombone back. I'm not interested in other women.' We all know that Mary Dickin was with him, but who else was there? Someone else that he could have been arguing with."

"No-one else," said Timbers. "OK, the young man with the black curly hair – he could have said things about the trombone, but hardly about Archie's affair."

"Alice," said Slowly.

"Alice? Yes, she was seen in the yard after she fell from the fire. But, still, that doesn't make sense. Oh, my God, it does!"

Slowly smiled, still working with her pencil, her eyes still fixed on her drawing. "It makes awful good sense, if Alice didn't want him to get his trombone back, or to get his hands on her girlfriend, Bernice."

Timbers reflected. "It's a good case for murder."

"Which means I can talk about Ned and you," Slowly began, but the chance was spoiled by a stranger's voice calling up the staircase.

"Is anyone there?" he shouted.

"Somebody's in!" breathed Slowly, her eyes wide with alarm.

"A young man," said Timbers, sitting up in the water and reaching, in vain, for a towel. "No-one I know."

"Crikey. Hide me, quick."

"How can I, Slo'? You've pinched my clothes."

"Oh no!" Both hands went to the dizzy girl's mouth. "I've thrown them over the bannisters. With Ned's dirties. I thought they'd want to be mixed up together. Your undies and his." Then her eyes lit up. She knew what to do. "I'll get you some more."

Slowly dropped the sketchpad on the floor and disappeared. Timbers heard the bang of a cupboard door, the scrape of a drawer, and then Slowly was back. “Here. A skirt and blouse off an old WPC. I remembered Ned keeps it in the stationery cupboard on the landing. Get dressed Timbers. I’m off to peek at the man downstairs.” But seconds later, she stuck her head in the bathroom again. “Get Ned to tell you the story about the clothes in the landing cupboard.”

Making as little noise as she could (though with Slowly running up and down stairs, what was the point in keeping quiet?) Timbers left the bathwater and dried herself thoroughly. Her nobbly feet soaked the threadbare mat. It stuck to her feet and ended up twisted and kicked aside. She looked down at the discarded sketch. Slowly had barely completed a rough outline – there was no light or shade and no expression to the features, yet she had already burdened Timbers with a head and face that looked like Popeye’s Olive Oil. Tiny droplets of bathwater fell from Timbers’ thighs and landed on the picture like the first spots of rain.

“You haven’t got a thing on yet!” gasped Slowly when she returned a second time. “But you must be quick! He’s been in all the downstairs rooms and now he’s come up to the middle. Timbers, never mind doing up the buttons, just get the skirt on!” Again, Slowly covered her mouth with both hands. “Oh! My God! That skirt’ll drown you!”

Timbers said lightly, “Get another look at the boy, Slowly. Does he look like Buddy Holly or Hank B Marvin?”

Slowly mouthed the names without a sound, and, when she was sure she’d got them right, she nodded. She was shaking her hands in the air as she backed out of the bathroom. “You must do something with the uniform, Timbers. He’ll know it’s not yours.”

It was difficult to tell the difference between the blouse and a man’s shirt. There was no collar, no buttons at the cuffs and no shape where there should have been a bust. Sergeants’ tabs were attached to the shoulders, and the tails were long enough to cover her knees and most of her shins. If she had been wearing socks, the shirt would have reached them.

Timbers took one look at the skirt and dropped it on the floor. It had been built for an amazon. Three Timberdicks could have made themselves comfortable inside. However, she unthreaded the leather belt and fitted it around her waist (almost doubling it). She looked in the mirror, cocked a hip, ruffled her close cropped hair and said: "The girl's a wow!"

Slowly had been gone for only a few seconds when she came back again, grabbed Timberdick's hand and led her to the railway room. "He's at the bottom of our stairs, Timbs. He'll come up here next. Oh God, they're going to hang me. They'll say that I shouted him to death. I held an Admiral of the Realm in bondage and I shouted him to death. I'm to be hung for treason without Her Majesty's dockyards."

"No-one's going to hang you, Slowly."

"Here he comes! Crikey, hide me Timbers. Help me get under the trains." She crawled beneath the trestle tables while Timbers made sure that her dumpy podge of a friend was protected by the raffia curtains with green woodlands and sandy lanes painted on them.

Slowly's head looked out as Timbers was closing the door. "Can I choose? "

"Choose?"

"Buddy Holly or Hank B Marvin? Can I chose which one?"

"Slowly, who does he look like?"

But Slowly was sure that she couldn't answer at once. "I need to know if I can choose."

" Alright. Yes, you can choose."

Slowly nodded. "Hank B Marvin."

The intruder had returned to the kitchen before Timberdick confronted him. She was barefoot, with just an oversized police shirt belted around the middle and free and easy at her neck. She tried to keep out of sight until the last minute, for maximum sexy impact. Yet he made little of her tantalizing appearance. When he said, "The door was open, Serge," he could have been talking to a dowdy shopkeeper who had spied him fingering the stock. He slapped his lanky arms to his sides and explained, "I know that I shouldn't have walked in but I did. I've not touched anything."

Straightaway, Timberdick corrected him. "I'm not a policewoman." But he didn't take it in.

Yes, he looked like Buddy Holly. He had a similar frame and head of hair. He wore the right type of spectacles, and trousers that, like Buddy Holly's, were slightly too long. But it was the show-biz edge to his bearing that made the comparison so strong. His head turned to every noise, and his smile could change in just a second. He acted as if he always expected to be photographed. He had Holly's eagerness of expression, the same wanting to perform and, when he spoke, Timbers sensed that he wanted to take his listeners with him. What he couldn't do, Timbers learned, was concentrate on what was being said to him.

"I was looking for one of your constables," he said.

"I must explain," said Timbers.

"You've no need," he said without a hint of amusement at her skimpy clothes. "I caught you in the bath and you've dressed quickly."

"No. Worse than that. I shouldn't be wearing this uniform."

"Obviously. It's far too big for you. You've had to borrow the shirt from a colleague."

"No. You don't undersand. I'm not a policewoman."

But he still didn't get it. "I'm looking for Ned Machray," he said.

"Ned's in hospital," she explained. "I don't think we'll see him till later in the week. The old windbag will try and get a couple of days laid up with people running around after him. Lazy bugger."

"I thought I might find a caretaker or someone. This is the home of the Police Dance Orchestra, isn't it?"

Timberdick put her fingers to her nose and pretended to stifle a snigger. "If it's got a home, this is it. They rehearse here on Thursdays in one of the old classrooms upstairs and some of their gear is stowed in the back rooms."

"And the band bus?" he added hopefully. "I saw it through the garage window."

"The old charabanc, you mean. It's for taking the drums in, since they ruined the first set in their car boots."

"This house, Serge?" He was looking at a corner of wallpaper, faded to a yellow. "It used to be a section dormitory or something?"

She shook her head. "A police school, years ago. Ned's got an apartment on the top floor but he gives himself the run of the place. Look, you've got things wrong. I'm only wearing this uniform because my own clothes are in the wash."

"You're Timberdick, aren't you? I've heard people talk."

"I'm sure you have."

"You're his girlfriend. I didn't realise that you were both in the force."

"I'm not," she insisted. "You've misunderstood. It's my fault but I've tried to explain."

"No, really. It's none of my business. You live here together?"

Timberdick replied with a frankness that surprised her. "He's asked me to marry him three times and I've proposed twice but we're still not engaged. 'Waiting.' That's about how things are. We're waiting and seeing."

"Ah well, that's a yes, then. Every child knows that when mother says, 'We'll see,' she means yes." He offered a hand but Timberdick did nothing with it. "My name's Melvin Parrot. Please to meet you, Serge."

This time, Timberdick didn't insist that she wasn't a policewoman. "Stick yourself on a chair and we'll help ourselves to some of Ned's coffee," she said.

"Sergeant Moreton says that I'm not to talk to you about the murder."

"That sounds like a Stand-by Moreton message, alright," she smiled.

Still on his feet, he said, "Sergeant Timberdick, I'm looking for my father's trombone. I've been searching since 1959 and just recently I've been so close. So close, but it's always slipped away. I'd heard that the police trombonist played it, so I went to last night's carol concert and I was going to meet him backstage and offer some good money for it. I mean, very good money, considering it's rightfully mine in the first place. Well, no." He paused so that he could look shame-faced. "That's not strictly true. About it being mine, I mean. But I do have a good claim on it. Anyway, then I heard that it had been stolen and Constable Ned Machray was chasing after it. Then there was the fire, of course." He pulled a chair from the breakfast table and sat down. "I was hoping that Mr Machray managed to retrieve it before the pub burned down or, who knows, he might have found it in the wreckage."

Timberdick bent down to nose in my fridge.

"Oh my God," she complained, her voice slowed down by disbelief. "Oh my God."

Some orange segments had been taken from the carton and housed in a old cheese pot.

"Oh my God."

The remnants of cheese had grown mouldy. The growth had wrapped itself around the flesh of the oranges and looked ready to sprout legs.

"Oh my God. I mean, he's a policeman, for God's sake." She left the fridge and turned her attention to the kettle and coffee cups. "Don't they give them training? Don't they put them in uniform and inspect them when they make their beds? He's a lazy fat pig. A lump of lard. We all know that. He treats a girl like muck and he is so much in love with himself. But this is the absolute bottom. Don't you tell me off, Ned Machray, for wearing last week's bra or sleeping in my knickers. Just don't dare, that's all. Or wiping up my gravy with my little finger." She turned to the visitor. "Have you been upstairs?"

"I'm afraid I have. I shouted first. To see if anyone ..."

"You saw his dirty socks and underpants at the bottom of the staircase?"

"Well, yes. I'm afraid, yes. I think I did see them."

"I mean, everyone knows I'm a dirty cow. It's expected. But he's old enough to be my dad, you know. You'd think he'd set an example. It's not much to ask." She brought two mugs of coffee to the table.

"Tell me about Connie Freya," he asked.

When Timberdick sat down, she sat on the shirt tail, and the tension tugged at the shirt around her shoulders and across her front. She shifted a little. Then, what the hell, she pulled the shirt tail free and sat her bare bottom on the cold seat of the whicker chair.

She wriggled and sniggered. The visitor watched it all from the other side of the table but saw nothing saucy in it.

"Connie used to live round here," Timbers said. "She murdered a young girl during the war and got away with it for twenty years. Then one of the tarts on Goodladies Road started to ask questions."

"Yvonne Young?"

Timbers nodded. "So Connie done her in as well."

"And you solved the crime?"

"Connie blames a lot of people but, yes, I was part of it. She always was a couple of coppers short of the full shilling but no-one saw it. Or perhaps we saw it but didn't say anything." She asked, "How do you know about Connie?"

"I used to have tea with her on the prison farm. In secret, of course. I've surveyed most of the old airfields, as part of my search. That's what Connie's prison used to be in the war. An aerodrome. She made tea for people in the farm office, and when she was alone, she made tea for me. It was Connie who told me about Glenn Miller's trombone being in the Curiosity Shop."

"Glenn Miller's nothing to do with anything round here. Unless you know different." She supped her coffee. "Now, you tell me about this frigging trombone. Worth having, is it?"

"It is for me."

"Famous, is it?"

"Not exactly. Sort of, notorious. It was my dad's. He couldn't play it very well and he told my mum that, if anything happened to him with all the fighting and bombing, she was to give the trombone who someone who would do it justice. A proper player, you see. Dad died in 1942 and I wasn't born until 1946 and, by that time, Mum had given it to Glenn Miller."

Timberdick saw the immediate implausibility of the story but it was delivered so easily that she didn't object.

He continued. "Then, after the film came out, I heard stories that the trombone had found its way back to England and I set about tracking it down."

He leaned forward and seemed to study her face for a few seconds. Timbers thought, 'At last, he's curious.' She put her head to one side and tried to look coy. He brought his fingers to his mouth, touching the words that were on the tip of his tongue, and when Timbers allowed her two protrudent teeth to peep over her bottom lip, he seemed to lean forward some more.

"Where is the old spice cellar?" he asked.

Timbers sighed crossly. "It closed, years ago."

"Only The Hoboken Arms Jazzband is supposed to be using it."

"The spice cellar isn't a night club," she explained. "It's just what it says, a cellar warehouse. I'm sorry, but you mustn't believe what you hear around here. The Hoboken never had a band. They put on some 1920s nights with a stripper and a group of the lads played behind her. Lemon Gimlet on piano, Peach on drums with Gus Brough, the Navy's best fiddle player. But it was never a proper band and they never had a trombonist."[2]

Timberdick left him at the table. She walked to the sink and leaned backwards against the draining-board. Her legs were on show and everything else was pushed forward. "So," she said, slowly, and put her favourite fingernail into her mouth. "You knew that Archie Dickin didn't want to sell his trombone but you've come round here hoping to get it."

"Things have changed. He's dead." It was a straight answer, unbothered by any of Timbers' attempts at provocation.

"Stealing from a corpse?"

---

[2] Here, I am relying on Timberdick's account of the conversation. She has always insisted that she carefully listed the names of musicians and, for years, that prompted enthusiasts to believe that Mr Parrot was behind the unauthorised release of the jazz band's Christmas broadcast. The sleeve of the bootleg EP provided a discography that matched the information offered by Timberdick, in the kitchen at Shooter's Grove, three days before the recording. (She was talking off the top of her head. She knew little or nothing about The Hoboken Arms' Jazz Band.) Any one listening to the four tracks would realise that no fiddle player or pianist took part in the show. The phoney listing was so wide of the mark that the Shooter's Grove conversation seemed the only possible origin.

"No not at all. I'm buying something from his widow. It's completely different."

"Most of your story sounds like nonsense," she said.

He nodded. "I saw the look on your face when I said that my father died two years before I was born. Do you know, I was seventeen before I saw anything peculiar in that. The way my mother explained it, Dad needed a son more than I needed a father. She said she could have found scores of fathers for me; she was quite goodlooking, my mother, and always sought after. But she had only one child who could be a son for my dad. So, she sort of adopted me to him."

"And your real father?"

"I've never needed to know. The father that I heard about was all that I needed."

"I see. It's like, being adopted by the dead. An interesting set of thoughts. I'll mention it to my curate, the next time I see him. He's always mixing himself up in questions of that sort."

"You've got your own curate?"

Timberdick laughed. "I'm a prostitute. And where there's a prostitute, a clergyman's not far behind."

NINE

Christmas Presents

The last Tuesday before Christmas, at ten o'clock in the morning, I walked out of the model shop with the carefully wrapped package under my arm.

"We're in for a drenching," said a young mother in a hurry. "I need to get these kiddies washed and back home before lunch time."

I looked up at the sky, heavy with storm clouds. Bad weather had been forecast for days and I saw little chance that we would escape it.

"We love you, Mr Ned," the mother promised as she pushed the big old fashioned pram between two lines of standing cars. I thought that she turned around especially, so that her raincoat and skirt would ride up a little, showing more leg, but perhaps I was just thinking it. These days, Shirley Beeston was always happy to make things a little brighter for me. Twelve months ago, I had caught her stealing baby clothes but persuaded the shopkeeper not to press the complaint if Shirley worked two Saturdays for nothing.

We waved at each other as she safely reached the other side of the road. Then she pushed hard up the Nore Road and I, making sure that the DeLuxe Electric Signalling Set was safely taped in its box, hurried into the street-market.

The place was teeming with Christmas shoppers and mid-morning tea drinkers. The trade runners, dispatched by antique dealers to find bargains offered in error, had been here at six but had given up long ago. Now, the lines were full of men on their own, dressed in over-large raincoats with pockets sewn in layers to carry any trinkets that they bought from the stalls or wanted to sell on. Dogs on lengths of string or no lead at all. Fat boys, too busy learning the trades of their fathers to go to school. Young girls, with their mothers' voices, too cocksure to think twice before speaking up. Two CID Aids, on the look out for stolen goods, kept to the other side of the aisle, worried that I might give them away. Sean's Molly spotted me from the snack caravan and jumped up and down; I couldn't get to her.

Miss Bellamy had brought boxes of old stock from her haberdashery and was doing a deal with the woman at the nearly-new stall. "It's good to see you," they shouted to me. "Safe and sound, yeah?" But too many people were in the way so I couldn't stop and talk. "See you soon, Ned," called Miss Bellamy. "Come round. The shop looks good."[3]

I wanted to reach Sean's record stall before the rain but it seemed that everybody wanted to talk. There was so much barging that I began to be concerned for the safety of the DeLuxe Electric Signalling Outfit.

"Plugs," muttered a little man in a secondhand Burberry. His collar was up, his hands were hiding something in deep pockets.

"Plugs?" I queried

"Black, white, rubber, plastic. All with fuses. All you need is the leads to put them on."

" 'Struth, lad. You'll get nicked. A couple of Aids are over there,"

"Two D.C.s? Gee, thanks, governor." He ducked down and he was gone.

---

[3] It is not relevant to the Naughty Wife Case but I will mention that Stand-by Moreton assisted Bellamy's Haberdashery for three months in 1966/7. Barbara Bellamy was re-inventing the family business and Stand-by offered to lend a hand with the stocktaking. He prepared, for Barbara, an inventory of the bras and knickers for larger women. He worked every evening in the shop, often alone, Barbara says.

Someone laughed. When I turned around, another old friend was beckoning me. "Here, here. Round the back."

"No, really, Horace, I've no time."

But the grandpa confectioner wasn't a man you could refuse. We knelt together behind a tarpaulin as he started to fill a canvas bag. "Last year's Easter eggs. Three for seven bob."

"You mean this year. It's not '67 yet."

"No. These are last year's." With every comma in the conversation, he dabbed at the centre of his spectacles, forcing them back up his nose.

"You mean twenty months old, Horace?"

"Three for seven shillings," he repeated, "and four monster bars of genuine milk chocolate. We'll say nine and thruppence."

"Really, Horace. I don't want them."

"You, Ned? You, not wanting milk chocolate? No, I don't believe this. I tell you what, for nothing extra, a complete set of Lyons Maid Train Cards. Now, you'll not see these around."

Several curious faces were peering over the stall. Russell from our local model group had his eye on the cards. I certainly wasn't going to let him have them, so I fetched the coppers and silver from my back trouser pocket. "Seven bob, we said."

"We said nine and three, Ned."

"Then put in an extra Easter egg. Nine and three, it is."

"Alright, my man. Four Easter eggs, four giant bars of Cadbury's milk chocolate and a set of railway pictures that they used to give away with ice cream." He pressed the sack into my left hand and shook the other. "It's good to see you, Ned. There's not a soul round here who wasn't worried for you. You're a bloody hero, saving those two girls, then refusing to go to hospital until you had sat with Mary Dickin through her dreadful news."

Thanks to Horace's special attention, I was now behind the row of stalls and able to make good progress to Sean's Records. There was a crackle of thunder, but it sounded distant enough to be in the next county. Nothing for us to worry about, yet. Molly, still too far away to hear me, pretended to be startled by lightning, then fell about laughing with a girl with ketchup in her hand.

"Sean?" I reached for the scaffold post. "Have you got a seat? I'm knackered."

"You don't need to sit down, Ned," he said. "Have you seen that Molly? I sent her for plastic bags forty minutes ago."

"She's with the hamburgers. I want to buy that record, Sean."

"Which one's that, Ned."

"Glenn Miller"

He started to flip through a crate of LPs. "Let's see, I've got a couple."

"But you know the one I mean. It had a black cover with Miller walking through the snow. It starts off with Johnson Rag."

"What about this one?" He pulled out a sleeve and admired it. "A beaut'. Not properly released until next year. 'My Friend Glenn' with the Ray Eberle Orchestra."

I didn't need to look. "It's not new."

"It is."

"I mean, the recordings aren't."

"They are," Sean insisted.

"Anyway, it's not the Miller Orchestra and it's not the one I was looking at."

He grabbed the two 45s that a housewife had chosen, wrapped them up, took the money and said, "Thanks, dear."

"I'll take this one too," she said with extra money already in her hand. "Mickey Mouse at Christmas. Yes, it'll do very nicely for our Sam's sack."

All the time, Sean was keeping his eye on two youngsters who wanted to pinch some sheet music from the rack.

Without looking at me, he pulled a second album from the box. "Well, now. I've got this one. Miller Music by the Modernaires. "

"Don't be ridiculous," I said.

Molly had turned up with two cheeseburgers. One was half chewed, she gave the other one to me. "I heard that you were alright, Mr Ned. I'm so glad. Aren't we all glad, Sean?"

"It's period," Sean argued. "1956, that's before the film came out."

"But it's not Miller," I said.

"Look properly at the credits, Ned. Willie Schwartz, Moe Schneider and so on. Here, is that my cheeseburger you've given away, Molly!"

"When did Moe Schneider ever play with Glenn Miller?" I asked.

"Here, Mister! You got any live Stones?" shouted a young boy from the other side of the alley.

Before Sean could answer, the mother called out, "Kenny, you get yoursel' back here!"

But Sean wasn't about to lose a sale. "Quick about it, Molly. Go through that crate of bootlegs and show the youngster the Rolling Stones at Wolv'hampton."

"It's not the one I want," I was saying. I wanted to discard the Modernaires album but could find nowhere to place it. "Look, I'm not sure there was snow on the cover of the one I want, but I've seen the photo in other places and I'm certain it's snowing in the original. The point is, Sean, was he carrying the trombone? He wasn't in the original but I think he was on the record sleeve."

"Does it matter?"

"I want to see if there was a crest stamped on the trombone. You know what I'm talking about, Sean. I want to know if Archie Dickin was playing that same trombone on the night he died."

"Forget it, Ned. Tell everyone else to forget it, too. The whole city's gone Glenn Miller bonkers – all because of that trombone. It's just a story, Ned. There's nothing in it. And anyway, you can't buy that record because I've sold it."

"Why didn't you say?"

"Because I knew you'd ask who."

"Who what?"

"Who bought it."

We both watched Molly, who had dripped cheese down the front of her blouse and was trying to scrape it up. The box of pirate records was lodged between her knees. She hadn't got round to trawling through it.

"Go on, then." I asked, "Who did you sell it to?"

"I can't tell you."

"You mean that Timberdick's going to put it in my pillowcase for Christmas morning."

"I think she was talking about stockings rather than pillows," he said but I showed no interest. He went to the back of the stall. "I've got these," he said as he rummaged in an old egg box. "78s. French, and not the full orchestra."

At first, I saw just the colour of the label and the dry, continental look of the shellac. Sean was holding them carefully, thank goodness, but his fingers obscured the motif in the middle, and I wasn't familiar enough with the records to be sure without reading the print. Molly was speaking up about something else and Sean was distracted for just a second. I kept my eyes fixed on the record labels. Gradually, like all good things that fate brings to us, the brittle gramophone discs passed into my hands. I got the tingle as soon as I pressed my fingertips on them. "Sean. They are gold dust."

"I know it doesn't say Miller but the chap who sold them to me said it was."

"Sean," I croaked, almost unable to speak. "Sean."

I looked at Molly. "Molly."

Then I looked back at Sean and said, "Sean. This is the Uptown Hall Gang. They recorded nearly twenty sides in France, after Miller's disappearance. Yes, these are right. Released by the Jazz Club Francais, by the Jazz Club Mystery Hot Band. But Sean, they're ..."

"They're yours, Ned, if you'd like them."

"Sometimes, you can find them on LPs," I explained. "But the original 78s are really ..."

"Are really yours, Ned. If you want."

I went red with embarrassment. I put the tip of a little finger to my eye to stall any tears. I couldn't believe that anyone could be so kind.

"Did I ever tell you about the time I dropped into a jam session in a pub during the war?"

He shook his head.

"It was January 1945. I was staying the night in a little country inn on the Suffolk border..."

"No, Ned. Come to think of it. I'm sure that you did tell me. I'd forgotten that's all. Really, take the records, they're yours."

I was pleased with myself. Four days to Christmas, and I was walking home with Sean's gift of rare jazz records and a sealed set of DeLuxe Electric Signals. Sean had hinted that a Glenn Miller LP would be in my stocking from Timbers and I was sure that Slowly had something particular up her sleeve. She had already spoken of Christmas lunch at her place. The rain was holding off so I thought I would walk the long way round, calling at the shops on the Nore Road, before getting back to Shooter's Grove. I wanted to find a present for Slowly, and perhaps something simple for Timbers.

Every part of our city seemed to be busy that day. Buses were packed and had no hope of keeping to time. Traffic clogged every junction. Even the lesser roads, where small shops and family businesses served folk from the backstreets, had no patience for vans that had to unload or workmen who had to leave crates or bundles in the middle of the pavements. Nancy Gilbert, wife of the sharpest second-hand dealer on the Nore Road, wanted to display some old furniture in front of her shop and old Mrs Hawkins was shouting that the Gilberts had 'no public rights in the matter'. The argument wasn't settled before a drumming rhythm leaked from an upstairs window and a teenage girl, out of view, began to sing along with Chubby Checker. In 1966, *Let's Twist Again* was already an old record but the dance craze had been so potent that Mrs Gilbert couldn't help joining in on the pavement. She put both hands above her head and wriggled in a circle. She had borrowed the movement from an advert for Fry's Chocolate; it certainly had nothing to do with New York's Peppermint Lounge. An off-duty soldier with amazingly long legs in thin trousers, sank into Nancy's tattered armchair and started to clap. A young girl ran up to her and twisted like a champion. Harry Turtle stopped his car at the side turning and cat-called through his open window. Because he wasn't paying attention, he almost ran over Bairnswood Beth. She was crossing from the other pavement, singing at the top of her voice. Then the teenager, cross that the old 'uns were playing up in this way, scratched the needle off the record before it had finished. Everyone grumbled.

"What you got there, Mr Ned?" Nancy called as I marched past. "My Christmas box, is it?"

"Extras for my toy trains," I replied, straightforward and pleased with myself.

"More likely, fancy knickers for old Timber-Arse," said Beth.

"No-ah!" drawled Nancy, already laughing at her joke. "Not for Timberdick."

"No!" giggled Beth. Then they both squealed together: "She don't wear any!"

I got as far as Goodladies Junction before Mark, the model shop man, caught up with me. "I see you've got a packet of 78s," he said. "What are they, Ned? What have you bought?" But before I could answer, he was unwrapping his own purchase. "The box of Sinatra Christmas records. I wanted them last year but couldn't scrape up the money. To be honest, Ned, when I saw you in the market, I thought you'd beaten me to it. I know, you can get them cheap on a Woollies LP but having them on 78s takes me back to the times when ..."

We had stopped in our tracks and were staring at the ruin of our old tavern. Two double deckers pulled up outside, just as they had always done, but it seemed wrong. Then I noticed that we were waiting on Timbers 'little bit of pavement'. Where would she stand now on cold or clammy nights?

"I found the old mantelpiece clock and took it home," Mark said, holding his precious records in front, making a pregnant belly. "It's scorched and twisted, of course. I thought I would let old Haraldson have a look at it. I felt that I needed to take something home."

I shook his hand (an odd thing to do) and said that I'd call at his shop before Christmas. "You're a good bloke, Mark." I crossed the junction and didn't look back.

In her little thin home on Goodladies Road, squashed between a run-down shipping office and a disreputable shop selling clothes and accoutrements to displaced merchant seamen, little Emily Dawson carried a tea-tray into her cosy parlour. She said, "That's because you don't know. How could you? You were only a child at the time." She set the Coronation tray on the table and laid two napkins on the thick woollen tablecloth. She gave a third one to Timberdick and, by tucking the fourth into the collar of her own white blouse, showed the table manners that she expected in her front room. She checked her fob-watch. "Donald will be in at four. Not that he minds me gossiping but I do like to keep him fed. It keeps him content."

"I want you to tell me about Polly of Blackamore Lane," Timbers repeated.

"Yes, dear. Please help yourself to sugar and milk, but do put the tea in first. It's easier to clean the cups. I prefer just a few speckles of sugar, no milk at all." She stood up from the table, saying, "No dear, you sit here at the table, but I prefer mother's armchair. Emily Dawson's parlour chair, for three generations now." She made herself comfortable, raising the teacup high in the air as she shuffled into the seat. "Now dear, how have you heard of poor Polly?"

"Slowly Barnes told me that she and Ned had something going, long ago."

"More Annie than Polly. Yes, it was Ned and Annie. Well, it would be 1937. The year of the Cathedral Close murder. Poor Annie Ankers was in the middle of it and she and Ned were close freinds." She leaned forward, nodding her little round head like a nervous chicken. The teacup rattled on the saucer. "You know all about Tom Ankers, don't you?" She went on nodding. "Yes, Annie and Ned."

"I really want to know about Polly."

"Oh, Polly and Ned. No, no. They didn't have a baby. Well, I mean to say," she started to cluck, "he wasn't in their loft long enough for anything more than a little spooning. Oh, no, her mother and father sent in the dog. But Annie, you see, made much more of it. She said – because she told fortunes in those days, Annie Ankers, I mean, and very good ones too – she said that Ned would come back and marry poor Polly. Mind, Ned would never have married her. He would have been pleased to rescue her, but marriage? No. You see, we all know that Ned will never marry a naughty wife." She sat up straight. "Something you ought to think about, my dear. Oh, that woman, she could tell a thousand truths."

"Who? Annie?"

"No, poor Polly. Living next door to Mr Dickin and his naughty wife. Why. All the comings and goings? I shouldn't wonder if Polly hasn't got them all written down in a book. And then, her husband not a dozen hours dead before his wife was full of tittle-tattle on Goodladies Road. That's what's naughty about it. So disrespectful. And after all that shouting. All that pleading. 'I'm only here to get my trombone back.' He begged her to believe that he wasn't playing with another skirt."

"You heard that?" asked Timberdick.

"Heard it? I saw it!"

"You mean, you saw the murder?"

"No, I didn't say I did, did I? I said I saw the argument. I was as close to the fence as I am to you."

Emily's man was home from the factory. The women could hear him working to manage his bicycle through the hall to the kitchen. "I wish you wouldn't," Emily called. "You know that Sefton said you'll spoil the floor's suspension." There was no reply that the women could hear.

"I should think that's all forgotten now," Emily contiued. "No-one would remember about Polly and Ned, would they? It was all those years ago. I only know the tale because my mother was out and about in those days."

"Did you ever meet her?"

"Of course not. What do you take me for? I never went down Blackamore Lane, not once in all of my life."

TEN

The Spice Cellar

For several days after the fire, Timberdick could not look easily at the sooted ruins. She couldn't walk through Goodladies Junction without snatching the taste of imaginary smoke from the back of her throat and down her nostrils. The rain had dampened the dust and made slurry of the ashes, and wet on the brickwork made Timberdick think that the stump of the old chimney-breast was weeping. "No more blokes will be coming out those doors for you, girl," was the grim remark from a lad on his Lambretta, as he wobbled along the gutter.

It was on the fourth day that she first noticed the old people picking through the debris. Their arched backs and their hands reaching forward made the shapes of black crows pecking at dead squirrels, but these pensioners were not looters. They were broken-hearted neighbours searching for momentos of the pub that occupied so many images of their past. A crooked policeman had once told her that no-one new came to Goodladies. Its people had been born here and couldn't get away, he said. That wasn't true. Few of its characters had been born on The Road. But it was how they looked and how it felt. And, it was the reason that Timberdick had stayed here so long. She counted on the doggedness of the place.

She remembered the despair, twelve months ago, when news reached the Hoboken that Widow McKinley had died. Goodladies wailed, then it went quiet, then it got on with its life. And Timbers felt sure that little would change this time, even if the old landmark, sometimes compared to an ocean liner at its berth, was no longer there. Soapy Berkeley would still be seen making his twice daily wander to the little square shops for bread, papers and cheap brands of tinned food. The impoverished bookseller would cross the road from the chippie, his greasy lunch wrapped in newspaper as he hurried back to his poky shop behind the chemist. He had left it unattended for only a couple of minutes, but he would be caught out one day. And would there ever be an afternoon when Emily Dawson didn't keep to the middle of the busy road as she bicycled to the picture matinee? She wore a black dress, black stockings and old fashioned black shoes and, always, her little dog sat contentedly in the basket on the handlebars. The scene never changed. Some people said that she had hoarded the clothes for years, but Miss Dawson wasn't the sort of woman they made jokes about.

Early one evening, when she had no thought of working for her living, Timberdick walked from one end of The Road to the other, from Goodladies Junction to the circus at the bottom where the buses turned. She considered the different shelters and corners, doorways and shady arches, and she decided that the fire would make no difference to one thing. She had stood on her little bit of pavement, opposite The Hoboken Arms, for twenty years. She had waited for the men – most of them good and honest, most of them caring – to fall out of the pub's double doors late at night. She knew how to stand in the half light, so that the headlights caught her long pale legs or the pushed out shape of her bottom, yet still let the men think that she was waiting in the dark. The pub had burned down but she wouldn't move away. She would continue to stand here and entice her blokes into the shadowy side roads. Rossington or Cardrew Street, sometimes the old Chestnut Alley.

Yet, there was a sense that the burning down of The Hoboken Arms pushed the red light junction towards a new chapter. "Widow McKinley never knew Goodladies Road without the Hoboken," Ma Shipley had been heard to say. Neither, Lillie Horsepool, Mother Dowell nor Gordon Freya. These characters, each an overbearing presence on The Road, would hesitate now before they'd recognise the place. Without The Hoboken Arms, the portrait had changed forever.

Timberdick had never visited the old spice cellar. The address was notorious because, years ago, two mariners with broken legs had been left to die in its caverns and, even now, tramps came here when they felt their days were up. People said that the flagstones flooded at high tide and that rats had the run of the place.

Her little figure disappeared from Goodladies Road as she took the stone steps down, one at a time. No light and no handrail guided her, but black brick walls, half as high as a house on each side, allowed passage for only one at a time. There was nowhere to fall except downwards, and Timbers reached the bottom with her arms stretched forward like a sleepwalker. She found the grab bar and was ready to push, when a gull screeched overhead. It was impossible to hear the call as anything but a warning. She turned her head and looked upwards. A last look before knocking on hell's door. The high walls and steep steps made the way back look like a tunnel, an effect that did something to the natural light, bringing the stars much closer to her. She moved her feet, wanting to hear their sound on the wet stone. Then she leaned on the grab bar and the heavy door reluctantly gave way.

The cellar was much larger than she expected. It surely extended beneath several buildings, if not two streets. The ceiling, twelve feet high, was a pattern of scallops, with sculptured joists where it met the arched pillars that rose up from the floor. The place was empty of stock, empty of furniture, there was just an embedded smell of sea-water built up over years. The cellar was joyless and unforgiving but most of all cold.

When the clang of the door lever cracked across the room, I looked up and saw Timbers walking to the corner where Lady Brenda was sitting alone. I waved but I didn't call out because I was busy with the lady clarinetist. She had written a trick into her arrangement of *String of Pearls* and wanted me to check that the other musicians knew what to expect. When the band was ready to play, I stepped aside. We called this giving the audience to the band, but Sean had made it plain that the cellar wasn't open for business so there was no audience. Just Timbers and Lady Brenda, and they were thirty yards from me (the cellar was that large).

"Ned has chosen not to co-operate," whispered the Chief Constable's wife. The acoustics of the place were so unpredictable that talking in careful tones seemed natural.

"Isn't he frustrating?" Timbers said with just a hint of mocking her posh accent. "He makes a girl feel that nothing she can do will matter. I don't mind you trying, but you'll get nowhere. Girls with class never do, with him. Did you know at a superintendent's widow took him to bed, then paid him fifteen pounds to keep quiet about it. Tell me – because how would I know about these things – is that what you'd call style or no bloody style at all?"

"My dear, I have no wish for Ned's attentions. I meant that he has walked out of the safe-house."

Timbers nodded. "It was the DeLuxe Electric Signals Outfit. Chiefie, you didn't stand a chance."

I saw that Timbers didn't want to sit down. She hovered at Lady Brenda's shoulder. All the time, Timbers looked around, trying to interpret the place. "Christ, I don't like it in here," she said. "Ideal for public hangings, that's what I see in here. Cold and bare. Plenty of water and just the right floor for flooding over the dirty goings-on. Can't you see them doing it? Killing people in here?"

"Sit next to me, Timberdick," said the older woman.

Timberdick stayed standing. "What about you? Should you be here?"

Lady Brenda reflected Timbers' nod. "They're rehearsing a Christmas show for Sean's pirate radio station."

"That's what I mean. Should a Chief Constable's wife be in on the secret?"

"Oh, I wouldn't worry about that. You never know who's behind what, these days. No, I'm here so that I can keep an eye on Ned."

"Touching."

"And because I knew you'd be here." Lady Brenda waited for Timbers to meet her eye, then nodded again."I need your help, Timberdick."

At that moment, I spoke into the microphone. "Spotlights and celebrities welcome you to the Cafe Rouge of the Hotel Pennsylvania on the shores of Long Island Sound."

"No, no, no." Sean snapped off the tape recorder and marched towards the little squares of lino that we called a stage.

"I've always wanted to say those words," I explained. "Ever since I first heard the air checks."

Away in their corner, leaning towards Timbers so that they could keep their voices low, Lady Brenda asked, "What did he mean, spotlights and celebrities?"

"He doesn't know. He can't understand the words on the records, but that's as close as he can get. We've both tried to work it out. We've played the whining bloody music, over and over. It's like listening to my own bloody funeral." Timberdick pushed herself off the brick pillar she had been leaning against.

"Bad, isn't it," said Lady Brenda.

"Bad," Timbers agreed.

Sean stepped back to the heavyweight reel-to-reel recorder which he had set up on a collapsible picnic table. "We're spoofing the Christmas Day broadcast from Paris, Ned. Like they did in the film. Try to stick to it."

"But the film was wrong. The announcer didn't use those words and the band didn't play Little Brown Jug. That was recorded years before."

"Sean's right," said the woman with the clarinet. "With Glenn Miller, it's what people think that's important, not the truth."

I tried, "Good evening, ladies and gentlemen, this is the American Forces Network."

"Do the BBC," prompted Sean. "They'll like that."

"Oh, alright." I was fed up. The show was becoming a packet of lies that we made up as we went along. "Who am I?" I asked stupidly, emphasising my complaint.

"Alvar Liddell," suggested the clarinetist.

"It should be Frank Gillard," I said, but no-one listened.

"They'll like Alvar Liddell," she said.

I began again. "Good evening, ladies and gentlemen. This is Alvar Liddell reading it."

Snap went the tape recorder. "Reading what?"

"The news."

"But this isn't a newscast."

"But he always said it. Here is the news and this is Alvar Liddell reading it. It was so we knew that he wasn't a German."

Sean was at the end of his tether. He had spent two hours setting up the recording regime, taking account of the awkward acoustics of the cellar. He didn't need a troublesome bandleader. "Look. Forget the introduction. Go straight to the bad news. And you're not supposed to speak before the first note of music."

I turned to the band. I lifted my arms and, when the boys and girls were ready, I nodded. They released a sweet, well balanced harmony around b-flat. "Captain Miller cannot be with us this evening..."

"A matter has arisen that calls for reassurance," Lady Brenda said, more confidently now that the music made it unlikley that she would be overheard. "The Admiral's body has been found. He died naturally, if a little unusually. He fell, collapsed, at the bottom of a wrought iron staircase in the dockyard. Close to the Chief WRNS office. Actually, as close as a wrought iron staircase can get to the Chief WRNS office. He was found early in the morning, so one might be tempted to wonder what he was doing there. But there needs to be no more than wondering."

"Do you want me to have a word with some sailors? I'm sure I could put the right sort of story about."

"That's a little piece of my point, Timberdick. I want to be sure that you're telling no stories that conflict with the Navy's version."

Timbedick said, "This is the sort of place the Gestapo worked in."

"Pay attention, young lady."

"Why would I tell a story?" Timberdick asked.

"Oh, you're very good. Really, I'm almost asking myself, just how much does Ned's dear Timberdick know. You see, the doctor's evidence suggests that the Admiral's backside had been somewhat spanked before he died. We'll say spanked but we probably mean something less playful. A peculiar passion found in men, not unheard of. It does occur to us that he might have indulged his peculiarity on the Goodladies Road, from time to time."

"Yeah? Well, if it was done, it was probably done in here. This, here, is the place for it."

"I need you to tell me, whatever the rights and wrongs might be, that no such tale is worth the telling."

"You want me to find out?"

"Oh, you dear little falsifier. As if you wouldn't already know the truth of it. No, Timberdick, I want you to promise me that no such story will be heard."

Timberdick looked around. "You know, Lady Brenda, you can believe everything they say about this place. Tramps coming here to die. Other men being left to rot, left for rat food, who knows? Just how much filthy money has changed hands on these slabs, do you think? Just how many dodgy deals have been done?"

"Alright, little lady, you'll get one hundred pounds if no story leaks out. One payment. Once and for all. And you needn't think that you've been clever. I was going to look after you, all along."

By now we were half way through *String of Pearls*. Sean seemed happy with the recording and the band was tight. Then, as they entered the phoney ad-lib break, they switched to a note-for-note copy of the Squadronaire's version of the same song. Sean didn't know what they were up to. He wasn't a Miller expert and certainly wouldn't have recognised a Squadronaires' arrangement but the little jazz band was soon swinging in a way that had nothing to do with Glenn Miller. My feet were tapping. At recent rehearsals, I had amused the crew by producing a few seconds of tap dance. (Try not to picture it because I don't have the figure for it.) I could feel them encouraging me. I was in such a good mood that I might have made a spectacle of myself but, just in time, I saw Timbers rush out of the door. I left the band to their music and hurried across to Lady Brenda.

"That awful Soapy Berkeley was calling her though the gap in the door," she said. "You better get after her."

PART THREE

IN TIME FOR CHRISTMAS

ELEVEN

Goodladies at Midnight

I was out of breath before I got to the top of the stone steps and had to hold onto the brick wall for a few seconds. Timberdick wasn't in sight and, although I listened for the familiar pad-pad-padding of her running footsteps, I picked up no sound of her. I flexed my arm to get rid of the ache in my shoulder and, when I felt that I could go forward without seeing stars before my eyes, I let go and walked into the middle of the empty street.

Goodladies Road, past midnight, was sore in its shoes. The drudge of the day – a hang-over of exhaust fumes, heavy rubber on asphalt and the rasping smell of out-of-date and overloaded cables, made the thoroughfare feel like a place with a raw throat and grime between its fingers. The rain made matters worse. It was hesitant and not enough to wash away the dirt. Instead, it painted grey streaks down window-panes and across paving slabs and would dry to crusty stains. A dog was retching in the gutter, trying to throw up the grit from the back of his mouth. He was a ragged mutt, he knew that, and he knew that he was in for a rough night. Perhaps he felt another storm in the air. The whole street seemed at odds with itself.

The homes above the shops were quiet. Radios and televisions had been turned off and mugs of bedtime drinks had been drained or left to go cold. The only lights left on watched over landings and porches. As I crossed the junction, I saw a child looking out from his bedroom curtains. Harry Ainsworth, three storeys up from his electrical shop, had opened his dormer window and was sitting out on the roof. He liked thunder and lightning and he knew that they wouldn't be long coming.

Smee Ditchin was running down the road in her flat slippers. Her live-in lover had walked out three months ago and Smee spent most nights searching for him. The Ditchins had lived around Goodladies for generations and, in the daytime, hardly an hour went by without Smee bumping into a cousin or an in-law. But her walks in the night were something that she kept for herself. Was she up to no good? Many people thought so, but I wanted to believe that Smee loved this place and criss-crossing the network of streets and back alleys after dark was her way of keeping in touch with her own neck of the woods. Tonight she was in the mood to tell tales. "If you're looking for Soapy, he's behind the bins in Cardrew Street. He was on your Timbers' tail till Chestnut Alley, then he snuck off like the urchin he is. Behind the bins, Mr Mach. Behind the bins in Cardrew Street."

She had shouted so loudly that Soapy gave up any thought of hiding. As I turned into Cardrew Street, he ambled towards me. "There's going to be a storm, Ned," he said. His hands, in his pockets, pushed his trousers down almost to the point of dropping. "You know what that means? Every trollop with stains on her soul will want to hide from it. All the weevils and worms will come out of the woodwork. Vermin will scurry for shelter."

"Soapy, that's balderdash. Why are you out here?"

I felt his eyes studying my face. "You don't look well, Ned. Let's get Harry down from his roof. He'll sit with you in his shop, just for a few minutes."

"I'm fine, Soapy. Timbers is in some sort of trouble and I want to know what you're up to."

"Then at least let's sit against the bins," he said, already leading me into the shadows of Cardrew Street. "I don't trust that Emily Dawson," he explained. "She left The Volunteer at half past nine, much too early, but she didn't go straight home."

"You followed her?"

"You bet, I did. What's that old witch up to, I said. Creeping off early when her stout's not half drunk."

"But you shouted for Timberdick," I insisted. "You shouted, so that she'd come looking for you, then you followed her."

"Who says?" He leant against the side wall of Number Seventeen, produced some gubbins from his mac pocket and began to roll two cigarettes.

"Lady Brenda," I said. "The Chief Constable's wife."

He called her the worst kind of name. "She's got no business round here. Thinking she can mix us up in her own double-dealings. She's too posh for you and Timbers. I've told you both but you won't listen."

He lit his cigarette, the tinder making patterns in the midnight air.

"Why did you shout for Timbers?" I persisted.

"Because I want to be there when Emmie Dawson speaks to her, and hooking myself to Timbers' coat-tails was the best way of making sure. They're up to no good, Ned. They're in cahoots, those two."

I scratched the back of my neck. "I think Timbers is walking into a trap," I said.

"Silly. Emmie would never hurt her," he said. A landing light went on above us as someone visited their bathroom. We moved away. We crossed Cardrew Street, passed two streetlamps that didn't work and stood beneath one that did, close to the junction.

"Emily Dawson doesn't know half of what she does," I said, trying to get more out of the roll-up than it could offer.

Soapy nodded in a way that said he couldn't make sense of my comment.

"What's she up to?" I asked.

"I don't know what she's up to but I do know what she's got. A secret in the old Curiosity Shop. I saw her letting herself in, not twenty minutes ago."

"She's got her own key? How's that? No-one's opened the place up since Widow McKinley's death, twelve months ago."

"Stands to reason. She used to do the old bird's hair, didn't she? Stands to reason, she'd have her own key."

"Right, Soapy, this is the plan."

"Oh, I don't like it when you've got a plan, Ned. Can't I talk you out of it?"

"You follow the main road. I'm going to cut along the Secondary Modern School fence, then come up the side alley."

"Oh, I can't let you do that."

"And remember, we're making sure Timbers is safe, that's all. It's not an ambush."

"No, I can't let you go trotting up the school fence, Ned. You'll wake the caretaker's dog. You know how it hates you. It smells meat whenever you're in fifty yards of it. There'll be a right royal row."

I patted him on the back of his dirty raincoat. "Come on, Soapy. Get to it."

"Here, it's just like the old days, Ned. You and me against the world."

"No, Soapy, it was never like that."

"It was too," he protested. "Soapy Berkeley was the first bloke you ever nicked. We both had to pretend that I was drunk or the sergeant would have clipped your ear."

At that moment, Harry Ainsworth stood up on his roof and shouted for our attention. "The railway banks!" In spite of the cold, he was in white shirt sleeves and no jacket. He waved and shouted like the last man going down with his ship. " A man in black! Ned, he's chasing after your Timberdick!"

"Change of plan, Soapy," I said.

"There. Didn't I say it?" he asserted proudly. "Never make plans, Ned. They don't suit you."

"You take the shortcut through Tullet's yard. I'm going along the embankment."

"Oh dear, oh dear," he was saying as I left him in the middle of the street. "No, no, no. It can't end happy."

I had galloped to the end of Cardrew Street, fought my way through the brambles between the old railway arches and was climbing the wooden steps up the embankment before I caught sight of the figure. He was thirty yards ahead but making no progress. I slipped and slithered my way through the mud and rough grass, shouting "You there!" "Halt!" and "Stay where you are!" If I had been in uniform I would have drawn my whistle. I was so clumsy and out of breath that the fellow had only to wander off to get the better of me. When he called back to me, I stood up straight and rubbed my eyes for a better look at him, but I was startled by the roar of a four coacher rattling past, just a few yards from my head. I turned, fell on my back and saw the lights of the train speeding past me. Someone threw a package from a window. I rolled onto all fours and crawled through the grass. I recovered the parcel, sat down and opened it. It was half eaten fish and chips, not meant for me at all.

I groaned. I had no chance of catching the man now. He'd have a couple of hundred yards on me. Then I realised that I wasn't alone on the railway bank. I heard a woman cursing softly, nearby. The long grass rustled and twigs broke. I crawled half a dozen yards to my left and tugged at the tangle of brambles. Smee Ditchen was on her back. She was trying to put her lilly-white and free-thinking breasts back into her sturdy cotton bra, but the straps were wrong and, though her blouse was open, it was twisted at her shoulders. She pressed one breast into place but, as soon as she went to work on the other, the first one flopped out. Smee was muttering, worried and weepy, in the middle of the difficulty. To make matters worse, she had to stay on her back because her skirt was up around her waist and, if she tried to sit squarely, everything secret would come to the open air.

"Oh, Gawd, Mr Ned. I thought it'd all be quiet and private."

"So it should be, Smee." I had already turned my face away.

"Excepting bloody trains with lights on and fat policemen falling from the trees or what-nots."

"I don't want to bother you. I'm looking for Timbers, you know that. Let me get out of here and you can carry on, just as you were."

Then the bloke emerged from the deeper cover of the bush. His trousers were done up but his shirt was still loose and, for some reason, he carried his socks in his hands. He stood strong, fit and ready to fight, but I didn't recognise him at first because he kept his face away from the moonlight.

Then he grabbed my collar. "Listen, you old bastard, stop talking about me. Some bugger or other's always saying 'Our Mr Ned's been asking after you. He wants to know you're safe after the fire.' Well, get this. After fire, flood or bloody earthquake, how I am is none of your business. You've no reason to ask. Do you understand?"

"Crikey, Tom. I – "

"Tom nothing. This Tom Ankers is nothing to do with you. And you can tell your Emily Dawson that I don't need her tuppence-ha'penny either. I saw her squawking to that bloody mad woman, the morning after the fire. Telling tales about things gone by. Listen, you don't tell anyone that you knew my mother. Do you hear? It was years ago, before your bloody famous war, and nobody's interested. So just leave me out of your life."

I didn't answer him, so he said 'old bastard' again and shoved me away.

By this time, Smee was on her feet and tucking herself in. "I didn't know, Mr Ned. I didn't know that he was going to be so angry. I was only saying about old Rosie Ditchen – her that caused trouble for Tom's mum when we was both children. I said, she's no relative of mine. That's all I said."

"Shut up!" Tom shouted.

I slithered down the embankment, scrambling to my feet when I reached the cinder path at the bottom. I heard Smee shout from the top, "Leave him alone, Tom! Can't you see he's ill."

I didn't look back until I was fifty yards further on. Tom was still shaking his fists at me. Then another train rattled past and, I guess, Tom and Smee went back to work.

I sat down on a dislodged mile-post and rubbed my hands over my face. I was in a bit of a sweat and needed to get my bearings. I had wasted fifteen minutes on the embankment. I was no nearer finding Timberdick, nor catching the mystery figure that Harry Ainsworth had spied from his rooftop. By now, Soapy would be waiting for me at the Curiosity Shop. Waiting, that is, unless he had blundered in on his own. I had nothing to show for my efforts since rushing out of the spice cellar.

"Are you all right, old timer."

I looked up and saw a lean character with curly black hair and a nervous hick in his voice.

"I was trying to catch up with you," he said. "I thought you were way ahead until I heard all that shouting. The thing is, I've twisted or sprained my ankle. I can't have broken it, can I? My name is Melvin Parrot."

He offered a hand but I did nothing with it.

"Most people call me Buddy," he said.

"What are you doing here?" I wanted to know.

"I wanted to get to the Curiosity Shop but a fearsome hound leapt at me as I was passing the school playground. That's why I started running and that's why I fell and yanked my foot. I don't think I can go on, but I'm sure Sergeant Timberdick has found the trombone. That's why she left the cellar. I searched the Curiosity Shop two days ago and found nothing."

"How?"

"With Mrs Stand-by. She's got a key."

"Grief," I muttered. "If many more people get a key to the old place, we might as well hand them out at the council offices. Look, we're on the same chase, Buddy. You'll never make it to the old junk shop with that foot. I can help you to the footbridge over the railway track. If anyone runs away from the shop, they'll make for the main road or, more likely, this embankment. You'll be in the best place to see them."

"You want me to stand guard?"

"I want you to keep watch," I preferred. "We want to be sure that Timbers is safe. We're not here to ambush anyone."

He looked me straight in the face. "Constable, you've seen Archie Dickin's trombone. Do you think that it belonged to my father? Could it have been Glenn Miller's trombone?"

The guy deserved an honest answer. I shrugged. "I've been trying to compare it with a photograph on a record sleeve."

He shook his head. "That would be no good. My mother passed it to Mr Miller just days before he died. It will be in no pictures of him."

"But this is a reconstructed picture," I insisted. "It's been tampered with. Look, it may be, just may be, that the record sleeve shows a trombone with the same crest that I recognised on Archie Dickin's trombone. And, I don't know, I might have seen a trombone like it at the end of the war. I'm not sure."

"Then I've got to find it, Constable."

I left him at the railway bridge and made my way through the builders' yard and the loading bay of the old Co-op and into the twists and turns of narrow footpaths that led me to the back of the Curiosity Shop.

Emily Dawson was waiting in the alley and came trotting up to me as soon as I turned into the little paved square at the side of the shop.

"Oh, thank goodness it's you, PC Machray. I don't think I would have been able to tell anyone else. I mean, who do you call? You can't, can you, call the police and say there's a ghost in Widow McKinley's Curiosity Shop? What if they said, 'It's nothing to do with us, madam. Not ghosts, madam, only crime and stray dogs.' I think they'd be within their rights. To say that. If you ask me, PC Machray, I think it's the old widow herself come back to haunt us. Didn't she say that she would?"

"Miss Dawson, Maggie McKinley has been dead for a year. I went to her funeral."

"Then why's no-one cleared the stock from her shop? Tell me that. Well, I'll tell you. Because everyone knows there's trouble for the man who lays a hand on her stuff."

"What have you seen, Emily?"

"Miss Timberdick came up the road and as soon as she got to the Curiosity Shop, she looked up and Widow McKinley shouted 'up here!' and waved at her."

"You saw her wave?"

"No. Well, no, perhaps I didn't."

"So how do you know it was Widow McKinley?"

"Because it came from her bedroom, didn't it? Hooting and flapping like an owl, she was." Emily considered the words, then shook her head. "Like an owl on the Palladium stage." She thought, then nodded; yes, she was happy with the image.

"Emily, you've lived all your life on Goodladies Road?"

"Three Emilies have," she said proudly. "Starting with my grandma.[4] We've never got married, not one of us, so we've all been Emily Dawson all along."

"And you've known the Curiosity Shop since it opened?"

"All along, since it opened until it closed."

"Tell me, did Maggie McKinley's husband travel to France at the end of the war?"

"Old Bugger, you mean. Well, no-one's too sure what he got up to, ferrying refugees here, there and everywhere. But it was Bugger's best sister, Els, who came back from Paris in 1945."

"So, she could have brought the trombone back with her?"

"Could have, but she didn't."

"You know?"

"I do that, Constable. The Americans gave it to Bugger McKinley and it wasn't in France. It was close to the English fens and marshes. He'd helped them catch a spy, that's what he always said, so they gave him Glenn Miller's trombone to say thank you."

"Thank you," I said. I had solved a long-standing mystery. "Thank you, Emily Dawson."

I unlatched the gate and froze: Soapy was crouched over a drain beneath the kitchen window. "Get down," he hissed, shaking his hand. "And shut the gate. You're letting in the light."

I did as he said, and crawled up to him.

"Timbers," he said. "In there. With old Widow McKinley."

I nodded and put a finger to my lips.

---

[4] Only as far as you knew, Emily. Timberdick had heard stories of Emily's mother working on Goodladies Road in Edwardian times, and old photographs, found in the Curiosity Shop, suggest that grandma Emily was famous for burlesque, if not more. However, in 1998 the City Records Office sponsored a study paper about 19th century prostitution and Emily Dawson is mentioned in a police ledger reproduced in the text. My own daughter, studying local history, took this to be the grandma, but the ages don't add up. It may be that our Emily Dawson , sitting in her little thin house, was the fourth in line. It was Emily's mother who came up with the maxim, "Real people get murdered by families and friends. We get killed by everyone else." (See *The Case of the Dirty Verger.*)

"Widow McKinley," he continued. "Upstairs. Making funny noises."

"Soapy, I went to Widow McKinley's funeral last year."

"I don't care what you did then. I'm telling you where she is now."

My gloved hand reached for the doorknob.

"You can't go in there," he said, gripping my wrist. "You're not a well man."

I shook him off. "For God's sake, Soapy. I'm fighting fit."

"Then why'd you take so long getting here?"

"I can't explain now," I said. "I'm going in."

Soapy burbled like an excited child in need of a toilet, then held his breath.

When I stepped onto the threshold, a twist of cold wind picked up leaves and debris from the gutter and two twigs, no longer than matchsticks, stuck to my socks. Inside, twelve months dust coated the abandoned surfaces, embedding itself in the nooks and crannies and dirtying the windows. Cobwebs, as thick as old women's stockings, had grown and died high up in the corners. I stopped, listened, but no-one called me. Everything was cold to touch. There had been no heating in here for two winters. I hadn't been back since Widow McKinley's funeral but my images of Timberdick and her girls in this kitchen – or on the bottom step, or propped against the doorframe – were so vivid that I could find my way around in the dark. I moved to the foot of the steep narrow staircase and stood – my body half in the hall, half in the kitchen. I could hear no talking or moving around. No ghosts tonight, I thought.

Then I remembered that Timberdick used to keep a torch next to the dish of stewed prunes on the larder shelf, so I went back through the kitchen.

"Are you in there, Ned?" Soapy called when my shadow appeared at the little mesh window. I heard Emmie ask, "What's a dish of stewed prunes in there for? Who needs prunes in a Curiosity Shop?"

I stayed quiet. I lifted the torch, wiped away its dust and shielded its light with the palm of my hand (although, with the batteries so low, the dim light was unlikely to alarm anyone). I kept the beam down, passing the table legs, the foot of the old washstand, the pile of cast iron saucepans dumped in a corner, and newspapers, dirty and trodden into the wooden floorboards. Still, the house was quiet. Slowly, I let the fading circle of yellow light climb each step of the stairs. Its progress seemed to turn up a volume; what began as a shuffle and whimpers, became a sad whine like a kitten's. As the torch found its way to Timbers on the top step, I heard tears, then cuddles. Two steps down, with her head in Timbers' lap, was the escaped murderess, Connie Freya.

"For God's sake, Timbers," I croaked.

The woman wore a long raincoat with a second raincoat draped over her shoulders. Her shoes were too big for her. She had no nylons to cover the parchment-like texture of her legs and she had the wrists and skeletal hands of an old woman. A scarf had been wound into a twirl and placed on her head like a hat. I wondered if Timbers had found her, hungry and frozen, and dressed her in old stock from the shop downstairs. She sat, folded up and barely moving. Her face was always looking upwards at Timbers, with the eyes of a forlorn pet. I realised at once that she didn't respond to anything she heard or saw – she just went on gazing at Timbers. I had the bizarre impression that she was waiting to be fed.

"Don't say a word," whispered Timbers. "Is anyone else down there? Don't let that Emily Dawson see us, Ned. She'll never keep quiet about it."

I was climbing the stairs. "Don't worry. Soapy's keeping her outside. He's good with her."

"She's a frightened kitten, Ned. She walked off the prison farm and she's got nowhere to go."

"Back to bloody prison, that's where." I reached out a hand. "Come on, let me lead you back downstairs and we'll get her to the nick."

"No!" Timbers grabbed the woman's shoulders and brought them to her chest. "She's not getting into trouble for this."

"Timbers, she's a convicted killer. She killed your lover."

"Not in this state, she didn't. Look at her, Ned. She hardly knows what's going on. Look at her eyes, Ned. They don't see anything."

I remembered how Timberdick and I had gone to arrest her, on a wintry night in '63. Connie Freya had been expecting us. If we had been any later, she would have greeted us at the garden gate. She was polite and helpful, finding a pen when I couldn't find mine, and suggesting the wording of the charge. She showed none of her wickedness, that night. Then I recalled the fresh pretty face of her second victim. Yvonne Young, 19 years old and only two years away from home. I remembered Timberdick's faltering voice when she spoke of another murdered girl. Then: the twisted, ugly body of Timberdick's lover, beaten to death with an iron bar.

I had no doubts; Timbers' sympathy was misplaced.

"We'll take her to hospital," I said, "and we'll phone Central Police Station from there."

"No!"

"Fordham Street, then."

" No, we won't! We'll phone no-one. No, Ned, I've been working this out. Buddy knows the prison. He knows his way around the farm. He's been checking it out for weeks. He could draw us a map. He could take us there. Ned, we're going to hide Connie somewhere on the farm so that the warders can find her. They'll see it's all been a mistake."

I shook my head. "God, Timbs. Think what you're asking me to do."

Without talking, we looked at each other as we thought of the pitfalls.

"Bugger off then," she said, full of sulk. "I'll do it all myself and I'll just ask you to keep quiet. Keep quiet and keep out of the way."

"She's not coming to Shooter's Grove," I said, already giving way.

"We'll go somewhere else, then. We'll stay here. Better still, we'll go tonight. I'll get Buddy Holly to drive us back to the prison." It was nonsense, of course. We both knew that she couldn't do it without my help.

I put my hands to my head. "Alright! But if she comes to

Shooter's Grove, it's for one night only and I'll drive her back to the prison farm in the morning. Right now, I'm going back outside. I'll tell Soapy to keep Emily Dawson out of the way. Then I'll come back for you. Don't make too much noise, will you? We don't want anyone else coming looking for Widow Mac's ghost."

Soapy was no problem.

"Important business," I announced as I stepped into the alley. "I need a clear passage out, Soapy."

"What's this then?" asked Emily urgently.

But Soapy saw what I was about.

"Of course, Captain. We'll get you a clear passage. This way, Em," he said, taking her arm, and he distracted her attention by explaining the origin of stewed prunes as a trade sign for loose women. I heard him say, as they turned from the alley to the Nore Road, "Timberdick learned it from her Pontefract man and thought it would be a good gimmick for the Curiosity Shop."

Locating Buddy was more complicated. He had wandered away from the railway and I found him drifting through Goodladies Junction, his hands in his pockets, looking idly at the burned out shell of The Hoboken Arms. I got the impression that he might have spent some time tramping over the ashes, but I couldn't be sure. When I told him that we'd found Connie Freya, he was eager to see her straightaway and I had to hold him back. "My job's on the line here," I explained. (It was worse than that. I could go to gaol.) "I can't have people ducking in and out of the Curiosity Shop, like the old days. Not tonight." I didn't mention that Timbers planned to move Connie to Shooter's Grove.

Yes, we could easily take Connie back to the prison farm, he said. We could hide her where the warders would find her without difficulty. But timing was important, he said. Too late, and she might be left out in the cold, all night. Really, she needed to be placed in one of the seed sheds between three or four o'clock. I told him to book himself into The Volunteer for the night and I promised to meet him before breakfast. He went away, knowing only half the story, but happy with that.

TWELVE

Storm Struck

"The escaped convict is locked in the boot room, and your stern mistress is sleeping with her toy trains. It's like putting the children to bed, isn't it?"

It was a cute notion. Just seven days ago, I had been on the burning rooftop while Timbers waved to me from the road. We had hardly spoken to each other since that night and hadn't found time to be on our own. We had, separately, asked questions, listened to alibis and weighed our suspicions. But, like mums and dads, we had been so concerned about the rascals around us that we spared no time to check on ourselves. "How are you?" I asked.

She chuckled and made another joke about Slowly and the trains. It was Timbers' way of telling me she felt fine.

The stroganoff had been her idea, but she knew that I would join in the cooking before it was half done. Cleverly, she had fixed things so that we would spend half an hour working together.

"Do you remember the first time we did this?" she asked.

"Back in '63. I had my suit pressed and my hair cut and I spent all afternoon cooking something Mexican."

"Yeah, then I turned up too drunk to eat it."

"No, it wasn't your fault. The dinner was so bad that I couldn't eat it either."

She laid the kitchen table, then suggested, "We've room to sit on the back step, if we cuddle up."

"Out there, Timbs? You're mad. It's freezing and wet." When I heard myself spoiling her idea, I said, "We could put the oven on and leave the door open." She was already carrying the dishes outside, so I followed.

Timberdick was wearing a red jumper and jeans. They didn't meet in the middle so when she leaned forward she showed off the patch of soft white back that I'd always been partial to. I sat beside her on the step, a little sideways on, and, with a crooked finger, stroked the back very gently, disturbing the little hairs without touching the skin. It was like a welcome home message between us. Because her feet couldn't keep still, she began to make patterns on the dusty concrete of the path.

"We always come back to each other, you know that," she said.

I nodded.

"It's like we're permanent, a bit in each other's picture that we like to ignore, sometimes, but can't paint over."

I nodded again. "It's sort of crept up on us." Then: "Oh God, Timbs, do we have to talk like this. We'll end up serious and deep, then we'll start drinking – and in the morning things will be no damned different. Why don't we just ..."

"Why don't you call me Billie? No-one else does and it would mean something, wouldn't it? 'Ned calls me Billie because Ned is real and we are real and Billie is my real name.' Doesn't that stand for something?"

"Can't we just ..."

"You've asked me three times and I've asked you twice, so next time's yours."

I didn't want to argue, but that made no sense. "If I've done it three times and you've only done two, then it's your turn to make it three each."

"But your times were early on and my times were later, so now it's your turn"

"That's nonsense," I insisted.

She jumped to her feet and scuttled back to the kitchen. By the time I'd struggled off the step and collected the dishes, she was standing in the middle of the floor, with her knuckles rapping her hips, her little mouth stuck out and her toes trying not to tap.

"Look! I'm bloody offering myself on a bloody plate here!" She started to march up and down – three steps and turn, three steps and turn. Her hands were waving in the air and her poky-faced head was tossing about. (Oh, it was lovely to see.) "Do you want me to beg, do you? Think you're some lord of the manor, do you? You want me to grovel, that's the truth. For God's sake, Ned Machray, just ask me to marry you. Is that too bloody much for a girl to ask?"

The truth was, Timberdick looked so perfect in a paddy that I didn't want to interrupt. I said, quietly, "We agreed to wait."

"But how long?" She was an impatient child now. "If I'm waiting for a bus, I know what time it's coming. If I'm waiting for the rain to stop, I know when it's done it. So how long am I waiting?" Her face changed. "My God, I'm on probation, aren't I? You want to see if I'll change. That is it, isn't it? How could you be so selfish? Always, it's my life that's got to be different, never yours. Don't! Don't touch me! I hate you!"

She went to the doorstep and, keeping her back to me, said, "I can't find my fags."

"They're here with the kettle."

She started to tap her feet. "Tell me about this woman they call Polly."

"It was before the war. I had been a policeman for only a few weeks, when I was called to a broken down slum in Blackamore Lane. You won't remember the place because they pulled down what was left of it, after Hitler, and built married quarters for sailors. Polly would have been nineteen or twenty when I met her. Her folks kept her locked in a loft and sent men up to have their way with her."

"And you went up, did you?"

"Yes, but because I had to. I was a policeman."

"You didn't have your way with her?"

"No, but I only just escaped."

"Go on. What else?" she persisted.

"Well, that's all there is, really."

"Then tell me what there is, not really."

"Only, a few days later an old fortune-teller said I would marry her one day. But it was years ago, Timbers. Oh, thirty years easily."

"Well, you keep away from her, Edward. I've met her sort."

"Timbers, you've nothing to worry about."

"Good. Now tell me about your night with Mrs Dickin."

"There's nothing to worry about. I promise."

"So you didn't sleep with her?" she asked.

"Well, no. Well, yes. I mean, she slept with me but just that. We didn't make love. I didn't know she was there until I woke up."

"Oh God, Ned. Don't try that again. Last time, you told me you couldn't remember sleeping with three women in one night."

"Timbers, that's unfair," I pleaded. "You promised never to mention that again."

"And you promised never to not remember again."

"That time, two of them were hiding in Shooter's Grove cellar . Yes, I knew I was with the third one. I just couldn't remember how far things went. And it turned out that things didn't go anywhere at all. This time, grief Timbs, Mrs Dickin had just lost her husband. I mean, she wasn't going to feel fruity, was she? I think she just wanted someone to put an arm around her."

"Listen, Edward. You listen to me," she barked, jabbing a finger just inches from my face. "While we're 'waiting and seeing', you bloody behave, do you hear!"

"That's unfair —-"

"Don't! Just don't! Don't you dare talk about how I live my life. I have to work. I've got no choice." She dug her eyes into mine, waiting for me to blink. When I didn't, she snapped, "Oh, shut your face!" and ran into me.

I wrapped my arms around her, and I felt her go on tip-toes as she pressed herself against me. Her little face was trying to tuck itself inside my collar. Holding Timbers like that was the most complete feeling ever. She was right; she was a figure in my picture which couldn't be painted over.

"Who's your number one?" she asked.

Before I could answer, 'It all depends,' or 'It's not a question of preferring one to another,' she pushed herself away from me and, keeping hold of my hand, led me from the kitchen to the bottom of the stairs.

"Mine's Stand-by's wife," she explained. "Emily saw Mrs Dickin arguing with Archie just before he died. Buddy backs that up. He reported it to your nurse-maid, who told Stand-by. Yet, Stand-by didn't arrest Mary Dickin. Why? Because he fears that the truth would come out and he doesn't want that to happen until he's found a way of protecting his wife. He knows she did it. So far, I can't say how she did it or why, but there's a feeling in my bones. The way she's pushed herself into the line-up, speaking up when she's no need. I know when all the questions have been asked, Mrs Stand-by will be the murderer." She made me climb the stairs first. She kept close behind, blocking off any retreat.

"Lady Brenda," I said. "She's pulling all the strings. I can't see what her game is but if Archie Dickin was in her way, she'd have killed him."

We went straight to my bed, sat on the edge and, without kissing or cuddling, began to undress. (I always start with my shoes and socks, although I've heard it said that a gentleman would keep those on to the last.)

"There's something I can't properly explain," I admitted hesitantly.

"Try. We're good at working things out together."

Without making it obvious, I kept an eye on what was happening. Timbers' breasts spilling free from a jumper are not to be missed, no matter how many times you have watched the sport. "The night the Hoboken burned, I was looked after by a kind woman in clothes like a nurse. I thought that she could have been something to do with the church. Well, she lost patience with one of the police drivers and boasted that she was on the same committee as the Chief Constable's wife."

"Lady Brenda told me not to worry about her," she said, undoing her jeans. "She's part of her team."

"Yes, but that's not all. I recognised her voice but couldn't place her. I've puzzled over it for days but now I have it. Do you remember, about three months ago, I was invited to talk to a group of railway modellers?"

Timberdick nodded. "The All Women Modellers of Somebody's Bottom."

"Hazeley's Bottom. It's the name of a village, not a person. We discussed the problem of realistic compression, I remember, and compiled a useful list of hints. This lady was the photographer for the evening. What's more, another member of that committee worked at Police Headquarters. What if they all work for the Chief Constable's wife?"

"God, she got her bloody tentacles into all of us." Timbers brought up her knees and extricated her legs from the denims. The soles of her feet were as dirty as usual, and her knees and ankles had been rubbed red.

"Yes," I nodded. "Something like that. Not exactly what you said, but pretty much."

Timbers said thoughtfully, "Your nurse can't have known that the Hoboken was going to catch fire."

"Just so, Timbs. She's not a local woman and, probably, I was the only person that she recognised in the fire. That's why she gave me so much attention. But it doesn't explain what she was doing on Goodladies Road in the first place. It's becoming pretty clear that she had to be on some sort of police business, or intelligence maybe."

"Or working for Lady Brenda."

"But, you said it, they didn't know that the Hoboken was going to catch fire. Archie Dickin hadn't been murdered before she arrived. Connie Freya hadn't escaped. So why was she there?"

"The Twinwood Trombone," Timbers said promptly. "The latest talk of Goodladies Road."

"That's right, Timbers. That's what this is all about. Now, why would Lady Brenda be interested in the Twinwood Trombone? I can see only one connection."

She crawled about the bed. "Come on, slow coach, I'm ready."

"Towards the end of the war our two teams were at loggerheads," I said.

"It's in Shropshire," she teased, making a kiss with her mouth.

"I know. Well, actually, I ended up in a Suffolk inn. I had stolen some secret plans and the Chief's wife (except she wasn't then, of course, and she wasn't Lady Brenda either) ..."

"Oh, get on with it, Ned. I'm trying to keep the kettle boiling here."

"She caught up with me and took them back. That evening, a group of young Americans were playing Glenn Miller music in a back room of the inn. The landlord claimed that they were part of the Miller Orchestra that got left behind. Sort of, reserves. Reserves for a jazz group called The Uptown Hall Gang. I listened to them for an hour or so, while Lady Brenda searched my room. (I didn't know she was doing it, of course.) Timbers, I'm sure that Archie Dickin's trombone was there that night. It had a crest stamped on the flute, just like the one that Dickin played at the carol concert. The Twinwood Trombone."

"How do you know it's the same trombone?"

"Emmie Dawson said enough to convince me this evening."

"Emmie's a spy?" she asked incredulously.

"Hardly," I smiled. "Though I think she'd make a good one. No, I had got as far as this quiet village."

"The one with the pub?"

I nodded.

"Yes, well, you've told me all about that. For God's sake, don't start at the beginning again, Ned. Come on, trousers off." She gave a playful tug at my flies.

"All these years, I have never worked out how Lady Brenda found me in that pub, until Emily Dawson told me tonight."

"Go on, then. Tell me."

"There was hardly anyone about, just an old country copper – and an inquisitive codger with a bicycle. They saw me book into the local, and one of them telephoned their black market contact on the American base."

"He knew what you were up to?"

"He didn't need to. He just reported a suspicious character and Lady Brenda and the Americans put the picture together. Later on, the yanks gave him Glenn Miller's trombone as a thank you."

"So how did it get to the Curiosity Shop?"

"The old codger was Maggie McKinley's husband. Emily told me this evening that his nickname 'Bugger McKinley' wasn't a new one, at all."

"It is," Timbers insisted. "I invented it."

"No, he'd been lumbered with it for years. And I remembered what the country copper said that night. 'Don't worry about him, old bugger. He'll cause no trouble.' Well, that's what I heard. But now I realise that he'd put the comma in a different place. 'Old Bugger, he'll cause no trouble."

Timbers shrugged. "What does it mean?"

"It means that Ned Machray, Lady Brenda and the Twinwood Trombone were in the same place in 1945 and, in 1966, they're together again. But how does that lead to the murder of Archie Dickin?"

"Tell me about the night of the fire," she asked. "How did you end up at the Hoboken?"

"I was last out of the theatre, I remember. The others had stowed their gear in the band bus and old Deaners was ready to drive them back to Shooter's Grove. I had already explained that I would be spending a couple of hours in The Volunteer and wouldn't get back before midnight. I all-but fell down the stage door steps and only some fancy footwork stopped me from dragging my tux through a puddle. That's when Archie Dickin shouted me: 'Over here, Ned! I need your help!' You know how Archie liked to say, 'if you please,' after most things he said? Well, he was saying it over and over as I crossed the car park towards him. I couldn't work out what he was doing with the police Anglia from Fordham Street. He wasn't on duty, none of us were, and if he was driving the police car, well, some other policeman wasn't. But Archie didn't explain. He just said, 'These two WRAC dollies have stolen my trombone, Ned. Come with me and get it back.' Now, let's see. The concert finished at nine-fifteen so it would have been a few minutes before ten when we got out of the theatre. I remember Archie looked at his watch as we turned onto Goodladies Road. It was five past."

Timberdick wrapped her arms around her shoulders to keep warm. That way, she cradled her breasts and made them bigger, I noticed.

Then she rolled onto her tummy and pushed her head up like

she does in the bath when she wants to blow bubbles. She made a paddling action with her feet so that her muscly bottom rippled, just a bit. As if the clockwork inside was working well. It would have been a shame to touch it, I thought.

"How did he know that the girls were heading for the Hoboken?" she asked.

"I don't think he did at first. We were crossing Goodladies Junction, and saw Mary Dickin standing on your bit of pavement. She pointed at the Hoboken's first floor of bedrooms. 'They're up there, Archie! They've got your trombone, Archie!' I asked him, wasn't Mary at the concert? I had just assumed that all the wives would have been there. But Archie made nothing of it. 'She's spending more time on Goodladies Road than's good for her. God knows what she gets up to. The truth is, God knows and I couldn't care less.' That shocked me, I can tell you. I had no idea the marriage was in that state."

"You went to face Alice and Bernice but Archie stayed in the van?" asked Timbers. She leaned up, collecting my shirt and chucking it across the room. Then she went back to her swimming pose.

"He said I had a better chance of persuading them to give up the trombone."

"He didn't want you out of the way so that he could row with Mary?"

I shook my head. "No. He just wanted his trombone back."

"Let's not talk about the fire," she said. "It was horrible."

I didn't tell her that the Deputy Chief's note had arrived in the morning post, advising me that I was to be commended for saving Alice and Bernice. I knew what it was, so the envelope remained unopened in my knife and fork drawer.

"No, it's got to be Mrs Stand-by," Timberdick said.

We were both down to our nothings now.

"I want bells to ring, light to flash," she warned. "God knows, you haven't made love to me since A Hard Day's Night."

"Only the second time ever," I said.

"I hope this is going to be good."

"It'll be your fault if it's not."

"Or yours, for not starting me up." She rolled over, onto her back, and stretched out. With her awkward, funny face and her bony body with its white undernourished skin blotched red where its corners had knocked into things, she looked like an original from a peculiar school of art, a picture that daring folk would hang in the downstairs loo where no-one would believe the colours.

I nudged along the mattress so that I could lie down without banging my head on the wall.

"Here goes!" she giggled.

A deafening bang shook the house. It was like being in the chamber of an exploding gun. The shock tossed me out of bed and, in seconds, I was scrabbling about on all fours. Gradually, I gathered my wits. I remembered the sound of splintering glass, toppling furniture and a foot-stamping boot in the television.

"Bloody Slowly!" Timbers shouted, out of tune. "What's that girl done now!"

"Crike, Timbs, he's got to the damned tele!"

"What's happening!"

She'd turned chalk-white. She couldn't keep her head up and her hands, too heavy, were reaching out for anything to touch. I saw her supper come to her mouth. She went under my pillow so that she could spill it, decently, into the screwed up leggings of my pyjamas.

My head ached. Every bit of me weighed a ton and, when I moved, my blood hurt.

I heard Timbers say, "I feel ..."

"... Radiation sickness," I said.

I was sitting on my bum, staring at a scorch mark that covered half of one wall. "He shot a bolt of lightning at us, love. Bloody hell, you can't not take notice, can you?" I got to my feet and Timberdick laughed at my naked figure. "We'll be alright," I said. "We're going to be alright."

"You're shaking, Ned. Stop walking round in circles."

I dropped to my knees and my head went into a spin so that I was looking at every inch of the room at the same time. There was a cook's smell of burning but nothing was on fire. Everything inside and out of me was nonsense.

Before I could put it all together, one of the women came running up the stairs. "It's wicked, Ned!" she yelled. "I didn't know what would come of it!"

Timbers caught her breath with a yelp, and I turned round to see Mary Dickin in the doorway.

"Ned! Oh, goodness!""

"Help," I said, and Timbers threw a pillow for me to hide behind.

"Ned!" exclaimed Mary for a second time. "That hardly excuses you. What's going on?" She was breathing in and out of her mouth, going at it like a steam hammer.

I backed up to the bed and sat on a corner of the mattress. Timbers kicked and shuffled until enough eiderdown was down my end to wrap around my body.

"Mary, what are you doing here?" I demanded. "You can't just run into a chap's bedroom like this."

She stared at me, longing to say something, then looked at Timberdick, whose presence seemed to keep her quieter than she wanted to be.

By now, Slowly was in the room and Connie Freya's banging against the boot room door was shaking the plumbing from the top to the bottom of Shooter's Grove.

"Good God, Ned. Cover youself up properly," said Slowly, with something that might have been embarrassment but was probably pity. Then, when she saw the blackened wall: "What on earth have you two been doing?"

"We've been hit by lightning," I explained.

"Go back to the trains, Slo'," said Timbers.

"We're never that good, Ned," Slowly replied. "Cripes, Timbs. What were you doing to him?" She stepped forward.

Mary took a sideways look at her and asked, "Who are you?" with a turned up lip.

"Should I ring the nick?" I suggested. "I mean, it is their house."

"Don't be daft," said Slowly and Timbers with one voice.

I wanted to get my shirt and trousers on but Timberdick had thrown them to the far corner of the room. I felt safer, here on the bed, wrapped in the eiderdown.

"Mary, why have you come here?" asked Timbers.

"Yes, why?" I said.

"I don't want anything more to do with the trombone. It's brought nothing but tears and sorrow. If you've got it, Ned, I want you to take it back to the Curiosity Shop and let it gather dust."

"We haven't got your precious trombone, Dickin," snarled Timbers.

Connie was still kicking the boot room door. Slowly had retreated to the railway room and was working the whistle that I had fixed to the ceiling. Then I heard her shouting livid instructions to an imaginary duty engineer. And, for some reason, Timbers had started to count down from one hundred.

"This is a mad-house," said Mary Dickin, bewildered and nervous. "What are you lot up to? You're hiding Stand-by's wife, aren't you? You've got her locked up in the basement because you don't want me to find her."

I said, "For God's sake, Mary. Don't be ridiculous."

"What would you know about it! They've stolen your clothes and won't let you get out of bed. My God, I'm phoning the police. That's what I'm going to do."

"Mary, no!"

But she was already running down the stairs.

I clambered across the mattress and got the bedroom window open as she ran down the front garden path.

"Mary! Nothing's wrong!" I shouted. "Nothing's wrong at all. Everything is normal."

THIRTEEN

Return of the Fugitive

"Nothing is normal," said Timberdick, reaching for her clothes. "We've got to get out of here before she calls Central Police Station. Get dressed, Ned, and get your car out of the garage. I'll fetch Connie from the boot room. Then I'll call Buddy Holly. We'll meet him at Goodladies Junction."

Waking my old Austin Somerset so long before dawn seemed as foolish as jumping over fences on a horse with indigestion. I opened the garage doors, patted the rounded shape of her boot, then stood around with my hands in my pockets so that she could get used to the idea. The handbrake was already off and she always slept in neutral so just a gentle push was enough to roll her out to the driveway. The exhaust was so perforated that starting her in the garage would have been cruel to the mice. Besides, she could overheat so easily that I didn't like to run her standing still for more than half a minute.

I was selecting blankets at the back of the garage when Timbers came out with Connie Freya. "I've rung Buddy," she announced. "I said we'll pick him up in twenty minutes."

I explained, folding the blankets on the back seat, "You'll need to wrap yourself up, Connie. We've got holes in the floor and we have to ride with a window open, unless we want to die of smoke poison."

"I've made two flasks of coffee," Timbers said.

"What about Slowly?" I wondered.

"We could put her in the boot," Timbers suggested.

"What, and dump her off the end of a pier? No, she'll stay here. She can be our bit of untidiness. If CID turn up, I'll be able to explain Slowly away. She'll make things look genuine."

Then Timberdick looked me straight in the face. "Ned, do you think this will work?"

"Only if nothing goes wrong," I said.

We were out of the city by four o'clock and had the road to ourselves for the first hour. Connie and Buddy sat on the back seat with a travelling rug over their knees and a bag of toffees between them. "It's like taking the kids on holiday," I whispered, remembering Timbers' comment of last night.

Timbers cursed the narrow headlights of the Somerset and spent most of her time craned forward in the passenger's seat, complaining that she couldn't see where we were going. The car's heater didn't help; it left the windscreen misty or dripping with condensation. I remember driving through a small market town before daylight, when a night beat officer, wanting to go home, stood at the traffic signals at the centre crossroads . He walked into the middle of the road and waved us through on red. "I don't know about a holiday," Timbers laughed. "That felt like crossing a checkpoint without being challenged."

"We'll need much more of that luck," I said.

Timbers was sure that we'd need Lady Brenda's help as well. "Our plan won't work without her. I'm sure she'll take more notice of you, so why don't I take over the driving and drop you where you can catch a train into town. Buddy and I'll take Connie back to prison while you meet Lady Brenda and convince her to take our side. We'll meet up later tonight."

But I couldn't believe that Timbers would treat the old Somerset kindly. "Better if we do it the other way around," I said. "You go to Lady Brenda's."

So we found an out-of-the-way country station and I parked outside the booking hall. Timberdick and I got out, leaving Connie Freya and Buddy in the back. There were no parking spaces but we meant to be only a few minutes. I gave the keys to Buddy, just in case.

The London commuters were still in their beds and staff were sneaking an early morning tea break. The next stopping train wasn't due for forty minutes, so we took our time. I looked around for a chocolate machine, but it was on the other side of the track. We walked along the empty platform. I slipped my hand around her narrow fingers and, like that, we sat on a bench. It was a cold morning. "Cold enough for snow," I said, wanting to make conversation about nothing rather than something. "Now, you've got the times written down, haven't you," I checked.

"Ned, I can manage a train journey on my own."

"Don't forget, sit on the near-side of the coach. Then when you cross the old viaduct you'll be able to see the old mile plate from the earliest times."

"Oh, Ned," she sighed. "Be quiet about the sodding trains."

"I know, but I was just mentioning a point of interest. It's the only one of its type in this part of the country."

"Ned!"

"I know. I know. Now, be at the phone box in the old lobby from six o'clock. I'll ring you if all's gone well, giving you at least forty minutes to break into the Chief's house. If you don't get to talk to Lady Brenda, our plan won't work."

"I'm more worried about that car of yours. Will it make the journey?"

"Of course, it will. Deaner's said I can fix the radiator leak by not screwing the cap all the way down. I just need to stop regularly and give her a drink. And perhaps a drop of oil if the weather's wrong."

"You will look after her, won't you?"

"You mean Connie? She'll be fine. I'm hoping that we'll lose Buddy soon after we've delivered our murderess back to prison."

"No, you must keep an eye on him. And do you remember what we were saying about Stand-by's wife last night?"

"I'm sorry about last night."

"Don't worry, we'll be together before long. I was saying that Julia Moreton had pushed herself to the front of this case. I was wondering if it's because she knows something."

"She saw the murder," I reminded her. "Or, at least, the shadows of the murder."

"But Emmie must have been there, yet when she saw Mrs Stand-by on the morning after, she made nothing of it."

"Here comes your train," I said. It looked too big and noisy for the station, and only six of its coaches fitted the platform.

The heavy diesel chomped impatiently as Timbers and I approached the second carriage. She shouted above the racket, "People usually kiss on a railway station."

I said yes, but she was already on board and I said that I was too fat to reach her. I just squeezed her hand.

"You're a right bastard, Ned Machray. You do know that, don't you?"

Buddy found a 1938 AA book in the glove compartment, a grey well-bumped volume, no taller than a Pan paperback but thicker and in hard covers, and quite good enough to guide us to Connie's prison. It took another three hours. Connie stayed quiet in the back. (I don't think she said half a dozen words during the journey.) Buddy seemed pleased that Timberdick had left us and Connie was out of the conversation. He wanted to talk more about his quest for the mystery trombone.

"My dad wasn't much of a musician but he loved his trombone. Mum said that he always spoke as if it were something alive, like a pet dog or a plant that had been in the house for years. He made Mum promise that it would go to someone worthy of it if anything happened to him. In 1944, she was working in a pub near Bovingdon airfield when she heard that Glenn Miller was going to be at the base the following day. She wouldn't have been allowed in there, herself, but she fixed it for the trombone to be given to him. Dad would have been enormously proud."

"And after Miller disappeared?" I asked.

"She thought no more about it. She hoped that the trombone was with him when he died. Of course, by the time she told me, the story was different: Miller had definitely taken the trombone and had even played it. She always told me that Miller had my father's trombone with him when he crashed. Mum died in '53, five or six years before the film came out. That's when I began to hear stories about the trombone being in England. Somehow, it had found its way here or, at least, it had survived to make it to France. You can guess the rest of the rumour: if the trombone survived then Miller must have come through as well. People loved it. They fed on that story, Mr Machray."

I had several questions but I knew that I would learn more if I let him tell the story in his own way.

"I started to track it down," he continued. "But the more I found out about it, the more doubtful I grew. First, people spoke of the Twinwood Trombone, but my mother had left it at Bovingdon. Then I found out that Miller never visited Bovingdon on that last day. Still, the descriptions that I heard convinced me that the trombone was Dad's. Someone had packaged it up, labelled it 'For Mr Miller' and left it in a store hanger at Twinwood." He shrugged, "It could have happened like that. Bovindon has such an atmosphere, such a story. That's part of the difficulty. People want to believe that magical things can happen there. They make movies there now, you know. Proper showbusiness films like 633 Squadron."

Connie was chuntering quietly to herself like a child playing with her toy farm animals, or making shapes out of the bedroom shadows after lights-out. Buddy ignored her. He was talking carefully. Whenever I came to a junction or a village, he would pause, and wait for a clear road before continuing.

"I found out that the trombone had hung above a bar in a Bedfordshire pub for years. People even called it Glenn Miller's Trombone, but it was one of those stories that's nice to tell while no-one believes it. When I finally located the pub, the landlord knew nothing about it. But someone told him later that the trombone had been sold to your Curiosity Shop in the late 50's. I heard that two months ago and that's what brought me to your city. I saw Archie Dickin playing it at your carol concert. But is it Glenn Miller's trombone? Of course it's not, Mr Machray."

I expected the prison farm to be protected by a high fence and loud notices but Buddy directed me along a rutted logging track, well out of the way, and we were three miles inside the boundary before I realised that we were trespassing on the commission's land. "Pull in, under the trees," he instructed, when the first of the farm buildings was two hunded yards away.

Connie, who had insisted on burying herself under the tartan rug on the back seat for most of the journey, lifted her dishevelled head and peeped over the lip of the window. This old woman had the voice of a child. Now that she was on familiar ground, she injected an excited squeak into her phrases. She acted like a schoolgirl returning to the hen coop after half term. I remember thinking 'God, is that what prison does to a mind?' but I felt none of the sympathy that Timberdick had shown for the woman. For all my laziness and disloyalty to the job, I was still too much of a policeman to worry about the well-being of a convicted murderer.

"Listen, Buddy," I said. "If anything goes wrong, abandon Connie and run for it. I'll take the blame. It's alright, I've enough friends to keep me out of serious trouble."

But he wouldn't hear of it. "You and Sergeant Timberdick have helped me too much already, Ned, and you've both much too much to lose. If I'm caught, scarper. But there's one thing I've got to tell you before we go."

Connie was already out of the car, muttering to herself as she tucked in her dress.

"On the night of the fire, you were looked after by a stout lady, dressed like a nurse from an old war film."

"Yes. It's alright," I said. "We know all about her."

"Two nights ago, I followed Timberdick from Shooter's Grove. She called at Slowly's lodgings, then hurried down to the boating lake, where she met the old nurse. They took pictures for an hour."

"Photographs of the pond?"

"No. Photos of Sergeant Timberdick."

"Ah. I see."

"I hid in the bushes."

"Yes. Well, anyone would."

"And I could hear bits of what they said. Ned, they know

where the trombone is. Don't trust her, Ned. That's all I'm saying."

He got out of the car, took Connie's arm and led her away. It was a peaceful scene, nothing like a prison ought to be. I watched the two figures walk, hand in hand, down the narrow farm track. They talked, they bumped into each other, they even stopped to pick flowers. When they reached the seed hut, Buddy unscrewed the bolts from the door, put Connie inside with no fuss and secured the locks again. He went round to the side of the hut, peering through a window to make sure that she was content.

I realised that this was some sort of lunch hour but, surely, there should have been some warders or farmhands about? Buddy ambled back up the little hill, stopping two or three times to enjoy the sounds of the wet countryside.

"That's it," he said as he shut himself in the car again. "It's all over." It was the expression of a man who was retiring rather than losing heart. It was as if his search had left a trail of untidiness, and locking up Connie was his first step towards bringing things back to order.

We motored across the Essex farmland, keeping to the country roads to avoid the towns. Before dark, we ran into a dreary drizzle and I had to keep the Somerset's noisy wipers going.

"I don't think I shall ever find Dad's trombone," he admitted.

Part of me didn't want to argue but I was there to encourage him, I supposed. "The search will go on for years," I said. "Taken up by others. Distracted by false leads. And the story will grow with it. The myth will stay alive, Buddy. You could say that the Twinwood Trombone Mystery will live on. Who knows? For two hundred years, maybe."

"You make it sound like the film of The Maltese Falcon."

"Well, perhaps it is something like that."

The petrol seemed to be lasting surprisingly well. I tapped the gauge and it dropped a couple of gallons but then the needle flicked up again. I looked at the milometer and, calculating twenty-four miles to each gallon, tried to work out how much fuel I had left.

"I wonder how Timberdick's doing?" Buddy asked.

I asked him whom I shouldn't trust. The nurse or Timberdick?

"You didn't make it clear." But he just looked out of the car window. He'd had enough of the business. I could tell that he doubted any justification for continuing his trombone quest.

"She'll be in the warm somewhere," I said. "She won't expect my call until ten or eleven."

"You'll be home by then?" he asked

"Should be. No, I'm sure we will be."

"How's the water temperature?"

"A little worrying. It won't do any harm to pull over for half an hour. We'll see how we go." I checked my wristwatch. "We've a couple of hours to spare, Buddy, so I'm going out of our way. There's a country pub that I want you to see."

I hadn't been back to the village since the war, so I was foolish to hope that it hadn't changed. However, although one or two of the larger plots had been sold off and modern houses had been built, six to a close, the development didn't seem to spoil the countryness of the place. I took my time, coasting down the main street and looking for the landmarks. I saw the twitchel where old McKinley with his bike had hidden from me, and the cottage where I had heard the singing. The hedges had been replaced at the War Memorial, where the bobby had challenged me, and the seats were iron instead of timber. The inn was in new hands, of course. The walls were painted white and extra ground had been cleared for a car park. It was The Old Bear now but it had much the same feel. I recognised some of the furniture. Certainly, the beams and pillars were still in place. However, the couple who ran the pub were far more friendly than grumpy old Grangethorpe.

We were early for supper and had the small dining room to ourselves. "I stayed here in January '45," I explained, accepting the mince and potato pie from the schoolgirl in an apron. Yes, mine was the extra cheese. Yes, thank you. "Miller had been missing for about a month but, you know, it wasn't the news on everyone's lips. In fact, when the landlord gave me the latest gossip, I thought he was talking about Jimmy Miller from The Squadronaires. They were my favourite." I dolloped ketchup over the potato crust. "Still are, actually."

Buddy nodded politely.

"Well, Red Nichols is my actual favourite," I corrected. "But, out of The Squads and Glenn Miller, I preferred The Squads."

"I understand."

"Still do."

"Yes," he said, doing nothing. He hadn't even lifted a knife or fork.

"But my point is, people weren't all talking about Glenn Miller's disappearance. The Battle of the Bulge was going on and the V2 s were coming over pretty furiously."

"So what were you doing here?" Buddy asked, but I wasn't sure he was interested. I think he simply wanted to move the story along.

"I think I was between units," I said. "Yes, that was it. I stayed just the one night. The landlord was keen that I should listen to a group of American youngsters who used his back room as a sort of rehearsal den. He said that they were musicians who'd been left behind by Miller's orchestra. Buddy, I'm sure that one of them was playing your father's trombone. No, I can't be sure, can I? I know, it might be wishful thinking. But I recognised the same crest engraving on Archie's trombone, twenty years later. I've been trying to get hold of some photographs but," I shook my head, "it just seems impossible."

The tale amused him. "You want to believe it, Ned. That's the problem with anything to do with Glenn Miller. People want to believe the stories and they don't give up until they can argue that the truth fits the dream. You cannot say that those lads ever played with the orchestra or that their trombone is the same one that Constable Dickin played at the carol concert. And, even if those two things are true, nobody knows if Miller ever saw the damned thing. Who says there is any connection?"

I smiled. "No-one says it, except the tingle in my bones."

After our pies and puddings, we adjourned to a quiet corner of the bar where we enjoyed cigars and a couple of half pints. Buddy sat quietly and I guessed that he was turning my story over in his mind. I kept an eye on my watch, but when I suggested that we ought to leave, he said, "Ned, I'm going to stay here for the night.

Thanks for sharing your memories of that day in 1945. You know, I think I can draw a line under the whole affair. Perhaps this is as close as I get to the Twinwood Trombone, and perhaps it's close enough. Get on with your journey, Ned. You've much to do. But I'm going to withdraw from the chase. I'm going to stay in this inn and wrap myself up in its old ghosts. Who knows, I might even hear some Miller melodies in the air."

He came out to the car and shook my hand. "Thanks for all you've done," he said.

I wound the window down a couple of inches. (It had a habit of falling inside the door panel if I tried too hard.) "Don't be daft," I shouted. "I've not done anything."

"Oh but you have," he insisted. "You've helped me understand the passion. My father told my mum to make sure that the trombone ended up with someone who could do it justice."

I laughed. "Not me. I'm no musician."

"But the music's there in your bones. You said it, the tingle. I haven't got that sort of fever. If the trombone ever turns up, I'd like you to have it."

"Nonsense. If it turns up, it belongs to Mary Dickin." I drew away from him. I looked in the mirror and saw him wave as I steered onto the road. I heard him shout, "Tell her from me, I'd like you to have it."

I had a hundred miles to cover. I knew that I could make thirty miles in each hour on good roads (the Somerset wasn't built for motorways) but I was supposed to call Timbers between eight and nine and I wanted to be close to home before then. You'll need to fly like a bird, I told the old motor. It was like telling a chicken to take on the grace of a swallow. But don't forget, the chicken and my old Somerset believed they could do it.

I left the old AA book open on the passenger seat but the map pages were too small to be more than a rough guide. Also, the car's interior light was no good, so I had a torch wedged between the seat cushions. The rain started again as I crossed the Berkshire border and I worried that the headlights might play up. But it all went well. At Hartley Wintney, where my route crossed the A30, I found a phone box and called Timberdick. She was waiting on a street, half a mile from Lady Brenda's home and gardens. I brought her up to date and gave the all-clear for the burglary that was the next part of our plan.

"I don't like it, Ned," she warned. "Buddy shouldn't have given up like that. We can't keep an eye on him now. What's he up to?"

"He's not up to anything, Timbers. He's a romantic. He's always been a romantic. When do you want me to ring Lady B?"

"Give me an hour and a half. I want to have a look around."

The run down to the coast should have been easy enough but the heater gave out, leaving my fingers and toes at the mercy of cold air percolating through rust holes in the floor. I stopped, and searched the car for a pair of driving gloves but they had gone missing. I ended up stretching the sleeves of my cardigan over my knuckles to make mittens. But I was still desperate to get my feet warm. I stamped around the parked car for several minutes but it did no good. So I pressed on but, five minutes later, my eyes were smarting with the cold and my nose started to run.

I reached the city before the pubs closed but I was in a raw temper. I didn't want to risk Shooter's Grove – I had an uneasy feeling that Stand-by Moreton or some other sergeant might be waiting for me. (I still didn't know how Connie's re-introduction to custody had been received.) So, I parked the Somerset on the forecourt of Smither's disused repair shop and stomped, discontentedly, through the alleyways.

FOURTEEN

The Tipsy Naughty Wife

"Oh Ned, darling." Lady Brenda's voice had the high-twirling cultured tone that nice girls use when they are tipsy and others are listening. "Please, no drama. It's three nights before Christmas and we have the Lord Lieutenant." She asked carefully, "Why ever are you calling me?" Then she paused, playing the words through her head to hear if she'd got them right.

There was a party going on in the background. No doubt, there was a log fire, Christmas punch and the smell of something hot and nearly done on the stove. The shouts of "All done for fizzy!" and "Cigars for the ladies!" made my fingers and toes feel all the more frozen. It had been raining since six. It dripped from my collar, it made the backs of my ears sticky, and my socks were damp because my trousers couldn't keep it out.

I was phoning from the box at the corner of Cardrew Street, twenty yards from the junction. Evening traffic was passing the site of the old Hoboken. No-one slowed down to look any longer, but the buses, with interior lights like ferries on pleasure trips, stopped where the conductors still called: "The Hoboken Arms for Goodladies!" (I had always enjoyed the message of that play on words.) Across the street, Harry Ainsworth had opened his TV shop so that a Christmas customer could collect a reconditioned radiogram. They covered it with a blanket and tried to lift it into the car boot without a scratch. Harry's young son was waiting with a bundle of disconnected legs and a fascia mirror. All three were sopping wet. Joanie Ainsworth watched from an upstairs window. She was holding a heavy oven cloth, and in the cloth was a giant dish of home-made pie. I knew that the gravy would be piping hot, the crust would be thick and the pie base would be generous suet that would soften in the mouth like an old fashioned pudding. Oh, what would I have given for an invitation to Christmas lunch!

I had dialled the Chief's number three times and failed, and even the operator had to persevere. The old grey mongrel, who was waiting to use the phone box after me, gave up and trudged back to the covered porch of the mission hall. The Christmas ribbons on his collar were limp and their colours were running.

I stamped my boots on the coarse concrete base of the kiosk. "You've a small bedroom in the corner. At the top of the stairs and turn left."

"My Lord, Ned, how did you know that? Yes, we have one at the front. It has a round window, rather cute, that shows the sweep of our drive very well. I'm really rather proud of it." She knew that her toffee-nosed meandering was annoying me; I expected her to go on about the corgi next. The Chief's wife wasn't always so pompous. She was light-headed that evening. I was the audience and she was playing to it.

"Timberdick is sitting there in the dark," I told her. "You need to speak with her."

"Timberdick here! Good God, does she want to join the party as well? Miranda from next door has just landed, simply descended upon us on spec. You are all full of surprises. Gosh, you are." She paused, put her mouth close to the phone and sang, very quietly, "Gosh you are, Joshua."

"Aw, give it a rest. I'm sodding frozen rigid in here."

Everyone seemed to be in better places than I was. The Chief Constable and his guests were relishing hearty company and hot food, Timbers was upstairs in a centrally heated bedroom (and probably under the eiderdown) and Buddy would soon be enjoying his after hours beer in The Old Bear. I had half a mind to ask Len for a room at The Volunteer. It would be more welcoming than the draughty staircases and cold bedsittingroom of Shooter's Grove.

"Are you still there?" she asked. "Have you passed out?" (I thought I heard her hiccough.)

I said something impolite and very quiet. I put the phone down and leaned my way out of the phone box.

Almost immediately, Dave the Taximan pulled up at the kerb. "Have you got somewhere to go, Ned?" he called. His wipers clunked loudly in the night. "You didn't ought to be out in this."

"Archie Dickin's house," I said without thinking. Perhaps it was the promise of fresh bread, cut thickly with a carving knife and toasted at the hearth. The stray had wandered to the middle of the road and was looking at us with his head to one side. "Can we take the dog?" I asked.

Timbers came out of the lavatory as Lady Brenda reached the head of the staircase. She hadn't pulled the chain but, realising that she no longer needed to keep quiet, she went back and did it, then followed the lady into the small bedroom. Timbers had changed out of her wet clothes. She had found a T-shirt and denim shorts that Rowena, their grown-up daughter, had left behind.[5]

"Oh, you poor girl," Lady Brenda said, really meaning it. "You've had quite a night of it, I'm sure. Why don't you come downstairs? You can help Geni in the kitchen."

"I'm going to spoil things," said Timbers. "I'm sorry."

"No, no. It's me – I'm going to spoil the evening, I'm afraid. I'm afraid I'm going to be not very well and any man ..." she paused to stop a burp, "... with any standards will be thoroughly ashamed of me. Again. He often is, I'm afraid, thoroughly ashamed. What do you do, Timberdick, when you're going to be not very well? I don't know why I am asking. I've properly been not very well far more times than you have." She giggled. "I mean I've probably been ... or do I? I probably mean properly mean. Well, it

[5] Years later, Timberdick's daughter found these shorts and we were able to feature them on the cover of *The Parish of Frayed Ends*.

all goes to show, I don't properly know what I mean." An alarming hiccough, more like a snort gone wrong, came without warning. "Here, sit with me on the bed and tell me all about it. No," she put one finger in the air, then seemed to forget about it. "I must tell you. Poor Julia Moreton has been on the phone and I feel so sorry for her. Stand-by's been deferred for three years and she's convinced it's all her fault."

"Good. It was. Snotty cow, showing off her posh-faced arse like that."

Lady Brenda took some seconds to absorb Timberdick's reaction, which she did with an exaggerated swallow in her throat. "She wants me to persuade my husband to reverse the decision and save Stand-by's career."

"Deferred means what?" Timberdick asked.

"He can't seek promotion until 1969, even then he'll be three years behind anyone else. What do you think?"

"Rub Jools' nose in it. That's what I say. Showing off her — "

"Yes, yes, quite. Or should I just take Stand-by under my wing. I could let him be one of my willing helpers, one of my busy little soldiers."

"He's a bastard. Twisting my arm, like he did. And he nicks Slowly for nothing at all."

"So everything stays as it is, you think?"

Timberdick nodded. "Except that Julia gets to grovel."

Lady Brenda nodded as well.

Timberdick waited for the woman to settle herself, then began, "Do you remember the night in the jazz cellar? You made me promise never to mention the Admiral's early morning habits."

"Oh God, must it all come out?"

"Not at all," said Timbers.

"He used to visit that dreadful Slowly woman, didn't he?"

"Slowly's not dreadful. She's just very good at what she does and men can't cope with that. They forget themselves."

"The dears," said Lady Brenda.

"The loves," agreed Timbers.

"Why do we call her Slowly?"

Timbers smiled. "Because 'more slowly' sounds different when Slowly's her name."

"Ah yes. There must be a story, is there? Where is she?"

"At Shooter's Grove," said Timbers. "Four of us were there last night. Four women and Ned."

"Oh, my word. Oh, God. I need to ... really ... I think I do ... will you take me?"

"Come on, I'll help you as far as the door," Timbers agreed. "I'll wait outside. Here, let's put a blanket around your shoulders."

"Oh, God, this is dreadful of me."

Neither spoke as they completed the manoeuvre along the landing. Timbers gave the patient a couple of minutes to settle herself, then knocked and declared, "There's no need to mention Slowly or the Admiral's habits. But we need to make sure that something else is kept secret."

There was a second or two delay before the return message was delivered from the other side of the toilet door. "Ah. One good turn deserves another."

"Something like that," Timbers nodded. The noise of the party downstairs lifted a notch, then fell, as someone walked out of a room and closed the door behind them. "Tomorrow the prison guards will find Connie Freya locked in the farm manager's seed store."

"Gosh, how embarrassing, if she's been there all along." The toilet door opened. "No, I've decided that I'm not going to be poorly, after all. The blanket is very good though. Thank you for that."

By the time they returned to the corner bedroom, Lady Brenda had considered the implications of Timbers' news. "Has Connie Freya been there all along?"

"She didn't burn down The Hoboken Arms or murder Constable Dickin, and you know that she had nothing to do with the Admiral's death, so there's no need to ask any questions. What do you think?"

"I see. Like that, is it? I suppose I could make one or two phone calls, and being Christmas will help. Matters can always get overlooked during a holiday. Oh, God, put your arms around me. I'm starting to shiver. I can't stand girls who chatter their teeth. It's so 'boarding school and homesick'."

Timbers took hold of the woman's hands. "If I tell you who murdered Archie Dickin, will you arrest them straightaway and keep my name out of it? Ned mustn't know that I worked it out. He'll think that I've given you a name out of spite. Oh, when he thinks about it, he'll realise that the truth was bound to come out, but I'm not sure that will change the way he feels."

The Chief Constable's wife widened her eyes, her cheeks flushed and she fell sideways onto the mattress. Timbers looked at the sozzled figure and muttered, "That's you until morning. Bloody marvellous. Bloody sodding marvellous." She walked to the door, switched off the light and was about to leave but, with second thoughts, came back and lifted the body to a sitting position.

Pushing and bending, she got the rag doll out of its intricate cocktail dress and trim petticoat. She took off the shoes, folded the knees and rolled her to one side. She was spreading the eiderdown over the top, when the sleepy eyes opened. "My bra too, honey, and my tights off would be nice."

"Well, aren't you the wild girl when you're smashed."

As Timberdick completed her nursing duties, finessed by tucking the blankets up to the patient's chin, cars started to pull away from the front of the house and noisy business commenced in the kitchen."You really love him, don't you?" Lady Brenda was smiling, her eyes open only a little.

Timbers had turned her back, folding the discarded clothes. "I don't know." She borrowed a corner of the bed. "I don't know that I really want to marry him. I can even live without being his lover. But I used to be the most important person in his life and that felt good. Oh, a working girl gets that worshipping, adoring, pedestally sort of thing all the time. But with Ned, it felt that it was the right man doing it in the right sort of way. I'd like to get back to something like that. More, if he wants it. Not so much, if he doesn't. I'll take anything."

The front door slammed.

"Won't your husband come looking for you?" Timberdick asked.

"He thinks I'm in the garage with a traffic sergeant. He thinks we're having an affair. He won't make a fuss. The Chief Constable is quite a detective, you know. I take a phone call. I go missing. The explanation is clear. The Chief Constable's wife is playing multiplication with the police driver. Timbers, who killed Archie Dickin?"

"Three people were there to witness the murder. Buddy, Stand-by's wife and Mrs Dickin. First, Mrs Stand-by. She saw the murder done, though only in the shadows. Her story doesn't really help us, other than to say she didn't do it herself."

"Which we don't have to believe," Lady Brenda cautioned.

"Buddy heard Archie pleading, 'I was trying to get it back,' and 'I'm not interested in other women."

Lady Brenda nodded. "Talking about the trombone in the first place. And, in the second, it was the sort of comment a guilty man would make to his jealous wife."

"And, we all know that Mrs Dickin was very keen to recover the trombone. I think she was the most serious one."

"Yes, the most serious about that," Lady Brenda agreed. "So she is the obvious suspect. It's hard to think of anyone else who was there and who would want to kill PC Dickin."

"Yes." Timbers was nodding. "Mrs Mary Dickin. The first and the obvious suspect. Yet, when Buddy told Stand-by about Archie begging and pleading in the yard, Stand-by decided not to arrest Mary Dickin. Ned and I think that's important."

"But he took my advice," Lady Brenda explained quietly. "I said he should make no arrests until we found the trombone. I didn't want it to go missing forever."

Timberdick nodded. "And, of course, Mary Dickin as the murderess makes no sense. Archie didn't need to explain to her what he was doing at the Hoboken; Mrs Dickin knew that he was after the Twinwood Trombone. And he wouldn't have told her that he wasn't interested in other women; he had been forcing his affair in her face for the past six months."

"So who killed Archie Dickin?"

"Before I can be sure, I need to know why you're interested in the Twinwood Trombone."

"Oh Timberdick, that story would be too long for tonight." She pressed a hand to her frown. "I can feel my dizziness coming back."

Timberdick sat still, looking at the carpet, her hands in her lap, her feet neatly together.

"Don't make too much of it, Timbs. I'm sure it's nothing to do with the murder. You know, I can't even say when it did start. I want to go to sleep now."

Timbers didn't move.

"Something has been bothering me since our little talk in the warehouse roof," whispered Lady Brenda. "The question's not important but I can't get it out of my head. The exhibitionist who wanted to make love to you in the cinema?"

"Yes?"

"You took his money .."

"I did, and why not?"

".. and you kept your eyes on the screen."

"Hmm."

"Was that because you were saying no or because he was making love to you all the time?"

"Chiefie, find a night when moonlight's on the water and all the little ducks have tucked their heads beneath their wings, then slip me ten quid and I'll snuggle up and whisper the whole story in your ear."

Lady Brenda giggled, then quickly brought her fingers to her nose, as if to stop some champagne fizz. "I'm going to be not very well, again," she said. "You shouldn't ask all these questions. Mrs Stand-by, Mrs Dickin, Buddy Holly. Who knows? Let me lie still."

Timbers said distinctly, "Woman. I am not asking you to belly dance around the bloody floor. Just lie in your bed and tell me why you're interested in the Twinwood Trombone."

"I have to confess to you, Timberdick."

"I don't want you to confess. Just answer my questions."

"Ned and I. We made love in 1953." She lifted a hand, then realised that she could do nothing with it, so laid it back down again. "It wasn't glorious."

"Glorious?" Timberdick said it again in her head. "Glorious? Lady Brenda, if it had been glorious it would have been all to do with you and nothing to do with Ned. Now, the trombone?"

"Buddy was spying on the prison. It had been a base for the American Air Force during the war. He thought Glenn Miller might have played to the troops there, and people there might have heard about his father's trombone. Connie was working on the prison farm and Buddy managed to get her alone. He questioned her. He wanted her to find things out. They met more than once. It could have been going on for a couple of months. Timbers, is this really helping?"

"Carry on."

"Prison security contacted Connie's home police station."

"Stand-by Moreton took the call," prompted Timbers.

"How did you know?"

She shrugged."Ned's got a word for it."

"Symmetry?"

"That's the word."

"Ned knew nothing about it." She nodded. "1953, I'm talking about."

"That's why it wasn't glorious," Timberdick concluded.

"He wasn't even there."

"Bren, love. You're talking nonsense. Let's stick to Stand-by and the trombone."

"I went away until the child was born. Even now, Ned has no ideals that he's the father."

"You mean ideas, Brenda. Ned has no ideals, not anywhere, not in 1953, not in '66."

Lady Brenda shook her head. "None at all."

"Good, so Ned has no idea and Stand-by took the phone call. Carry on."

"Stand-by told me about it. My husband was looking to dismiss him from the force at that time, but I convinced him to attach the poor soul to my team. I told Stand-by that old Bugger McKinley probably still had the trombone when he died and, more importantly, a written provenance setting out the whole story. I told him to look for a suitcase full of old advertisements for Edwardian undergarments because McKinley had written the verification on the back of one of the sheets. By the time he got back to me, the trombone had been sold and the knicker poster had been thrown out. That's what he said, anyway."

"Unlikely," muttered Timberdick. "If I know Stand-by at all, anything to do with bras and pants would end up under his bed. And what was old Bugger doing, scribbling on the back of smutty adverts."

"Hardly smutty, darling. The model was a lady singer in Bugger's old village, and he collected pictures of her. He had a thing for her. He used to wheel his bicycle around the village at night, hoping to peep through her windows. There was gossip that she always rewarded his efforts with something to look at."

"But why?" Timbers asked.

"Because it's what men do."

Timbers shook her head. "I'm saying, why were you interested?"

"Because, by that time, I had learned that one of my agents was double dealing. He was trying to divert the trombone, get it out of the country."

"The Admiral?"

"The one you call the Admiral, yes. He convinced two WRACS to work for him after hours. He pretended it was very important, very secret, very likely to be good for them. Timbers, you really are going to have to help me. I really do not feel very well."

"Who saw Archie with the trombone?"

"Buddy tracked it down. That's why everybody was suddenly interested in Goodladies Road."

Timberdick persisted irritably. "But why were you interested in the bloody trombone?"

The woman sighed. "Because I remembered Ned's face when he was listening to the band in that village pub. I knew he'd love to have that trombone. I wanted to get it for him." She closed her eyes as she spoke, knowing that her explanation would make her sound like a schoolgirl with a crush. "I should be something special to him. For God's sake, I've carried his child, haven't I? I knew that if I could get the Twinwood Trombone, well, it would be better than any present other girls could give. He'd remember me every time he looked at it."

Timberdick nodded.

"I'm not your rival, dear. Really, I'm not."

"I know."

"You have Ned's heart. You really do. But he could never marry you as you are."

"I know. He won't have a naughty wife."

"Something like that." Lady Brenda tried to look comforting but only managed to look, well, green in the face. "Now Timberdick," she said, holding her tummy in place. "Who killed Archie Dickin?"

"There was another witness. I said that three people were near the murder, but there was Emily Dawson also."

"Emily who? Who the hell is Emily?"

"You've seen her. She rides a bicycle down the middle of Goodladies Road every afternoon and won't let anything pass. Emily said that she saw Archie shouting at his wife in the Hoboken's yard. He wasn't having an affair. He was only there to look for the trombone. When Emily told me, I thought she was just confirming what Buddy had said. Two witnesses to the same argument. It seemed very strong. But Emily's story was much more important than that. The dear old cow had the key to the whole business, though I couldn't see it at first. I was puzzled." Timbers shook her head. "From the start, there was something wrong with it. Then Emmie told me that she had seen Mary Dickin with Slowly Barnes on the morning after the murder. That seemed wrong because Polly, the next door neighbour, had told Slowly that Ned and Mary had gone indoors at midnight and hadn't come out. But that couldn't have anything to do with the murder, could it? Then the lightning struck Shooter's Grove. Slowly and Mary rushed into our bedroom and it was plain – absolutely plain – that they'd never seen each other before. They didn't meet on the morning after. So," she clapped her hands to her knees, "it's all clear, isn't it! On the morning after the murder, Emily saw Slowly with the woman she had seen arguing the night before. But it wasn't Mary Dickin. You see, Slowly had already told me that she met someone else that morning."

The Chief Constable's wife was trying to get to her feet. "Please, you've got to help me. I'm going to be ill."

Timbers steadied the uncertain shoulders as the woman found her balance. "Keep the blanket round you."

"No, it's all right."

"Look, what I said about Mr and Mrs Stand-by was all wrong. You must get them off."

"No," she said, shaking her head in a silly way. "There's no need for you to hold me."

But, hardly able to stand, she fell into Timbers arms.

The bedroom door flew open. Light from the landing flooded the room and made the women wince.

"Outrageous!"

The Chief Constable saw his wife in Timberdick's arms. He was confused, because the tart was wearing shorts and a T-shirt from his daughter's closet, but he could see clearly what was going on. His wife was in the buff, save for her see-through panties, and she was trying to hide her breasts by tucking them under Timberdick's chin.

FIFTEEN

The Arrest

Mary Dickin had rolled over in the bed and, when I got back with the pot of tea, her head was nestled in the dip between our pillows. "I knew you weren't a man to leave a job half done," she said. "When you stroked my bum on the night dear Archie died, I thought, don't worry, Mary. Ned will be back to finish off."

I was wearing Archie's pyjamas and dressing gown and a pair of his slippers with holes in the heels. I sat on the edge of Mary's double bed and settled the tray safely on the counterpane. "Do you want to sit up and nibble a biscuit?" I asked.

Her eyes sparkled above the stitched hems of the different coloured blankets. "No, I want you to come back to bed. It's my smell, isn't it. Archie said that he'd always come back because of the way I smelled. He couldn't do without it. Do you know what it is? Shall I tell you my secret?"

"I'd rather you didn't."

"Then, oh it was so lovely when you exposed yourself to me on the day the lightning struck. I know, you'll say you were in bed with that awful Trimblety girl but it was me you were showing off to. Don't pretend that it wasn't."

"Mary, I want to explain about last night. I came back to see Polly."

"I know. You wanted her to have that sweet lovely puppy for Christmas. Oh, that's so romantic, Edward. But I wasn't going to let her take you as well as the puppy. Oh, no! I wasn't going to let that happen again. She's a bad woman, Ned. That's why I had to entice you." She tried to breathe through her nose but couldn't get enough air in. She coughed, cleared her throat and went back to mouth breathing. "Buttered crumpets and hot milk on the hearth-rug. I knew that you couldn't resist. You're not sorry about last night, are you?"

Suddenly police sirens shattered the early morning peace of The Close. Blue lights reflected across the bedroom ceiling. For a horrible moment, I thought that the headlights of the squad cars were targeting our window.

"Oh good, it's a raid!" she squealed.

"Stay in bed!" I shouted.

But she was already looking through the curtains. "They're hundreds. All marching up Polly's garden path!"

I pulled her back from the window. "Hide!"

She screamed excitedly as she bounced onto the bed. The next moment, she was sitting on a cushion of four pillows.

"Get under the covers, Mary, and stay there. Pull them over your head and don't come out."

She did as she was told but, as I walked out of the room, her muffled words made uncomfortable sense: "But Ned, it's my home. I'm supposed to be here. It's you who should be hiding."

Lady Brenda was already knocking on the back door. "They're arresting Polly for the Hoboken fire," she reported as she stepped into the kitchen, "and the murder of Archie Dickin."

I didn't say anything for a few minutes. Everything needed to settle down before I could make sense of what was happening. But Brenda was in the mood to be in charge. She found things to do – filling the kettle, wringing a dishcloth, bringing butter from the fridge and looking for the cutlery. Thank God, Mary stayed out of the way.

I said, "Thirty years ago, a fortune-teller promised that I was going to marry Polly. I never believed it."

Lady Brenda said,"She was the naughty wife you'd never marry."

I frowned at that.

"Something Emily Dawson told Timberdick," she explained.

I supposed it was right. "But finding her again did feel something like fate. Timberdick told you, didn't she? She worked it out, then told you in the corner bedroom last night."

"Polly thought that Archie was cheating on her," she explained. "Not with his wife. That wasn't really cheating. But with your two girl soldiers. Buddy and Emily heard him pleading with her. He kept saying that he was only looking for the trombone. Then Standby's wife saw the shadows of Polly's attack on him. The following morning, Emily saw the same woman speaking to Slowly Barnes, but she mistakenly said that it was Mary Dickin. She didn't know any better; she'd just assumed that she had heard an argument between husband and wife. Yes, Timbers unravelled it all."

She continued, "The Admiral died under the weight of dirty thoughts. Mainly, put there by Slowly Barnes but we'll not blame her. We're pretending that he died at the bottom of the dockyard steps. Connie Freya? Yes, we're pretending about her as well. A case of Timberdick Wraps It Up, I rather think."

I looked out of the kitchen window. Troops of policemen were hurrying to and from Polly's shed. "It's the dog I feel sorry for. She'll be in the slammer before ten o'clock. Talk about Christmas Day in the workhouse. Poor mutt."

"What have you got on, Ned?"

"Archie's pyjamas."

"How appropriate. How very neat, they look. Just slipped into them, have you?"

Mary poked her head into the room, her chiffon askew, her hair in a tumble. "I won't be a moment," she said. "One moment and I'll cook us all toast. Let me get some clothes on, first."

"I better get dressed too," I said and started to follow.

"Oh, Ned," said Lady Brenda.

"Yes?" I turned to face her.

I saw her hand in the air, just a second before it crashed into the side of my head.

"Christ!" It sent me backwards. I fell over the breakfast table and dropped to the floor with a chair on top of me. When I came up, my cheek was already bleeding and I could feel the flesh throbbing under my eye. "Bloody hell!" I held a hand to my face to stop it falling apart. "Christ! Why did you do that?"

"Why? Because she would never do it hard enough, so I thought I'd do it for her."

SIXTEEN

Christmas Cheated

Christmas Day on Goodladies Road. The December drizzle had turned to a watery sleet, enough for young faces at windows to cry, "A white Christmas!" but the postbox at the junction wouldn't be dressed as a snowman this year.

Soapy Berkeley muttered and groaned as he trod his wet way towards The Volunteer. When the parish curate came trotting along the pavement in the other direction, with his coats and scarves and pullovers on his arms and two pairs of new boots hanging from his neck, and shouted "A merry Christmas, Mr Berkeley!" Soapy brightened up.

"To you too, Sir! Yes, a very merry Christmas to you."

Now that someone had noticed him, Soapy lifted his step and faced the damp weather with a grin. He tried to remember the words to a popular Christmas song, but he made a poor job of it. As he reached Goodladies Junction, he made up his own words to fit the tune and by the time he reached The Volunteer, he had decided that his words were probably better.

Mrs Stand-by had cooked a hot Christmas buffet. She had asked for white folded sheets to be stretched from one end of the counter to the other and, at twelve o'clock, dishes and saucers and huge round plates were brought out – packed with seasoned goodies for anyone to enjoy. The man with the braces and the man with his middle button done up were there, but they had homes to go to (and family Christmas dinners) so they stayed just long enough to say they'd taken part. Dave the Taximan left early as well. It had been Mrs Stand-by's wish to provide a Chrismtas lunch for that community of old folk who'd have nowhere to go now that The Hoboken Arms was nothing but rubble. Everyone thought it was a good idea and Len, the publican, had put the word around. And, in the end , with The Volunteer being a smaller pub than the spreading Hoboken and there being no better pubs in the district and no noise but their own, the pensioners agreed that Mrs Stand-by had come up with the cosiest and loveliest, traditional Christmas lunch since the war. Soapy got to sing his song, the fogey from the run-down bookshop told some stories, and Emily Dawson ruled that tinsel should be draped over the naughty picture of Timberdick Woodcock. "She's already entered into too much spirit!"

Betty 'Slowly' Barnes had invited Timberdick and me for Christmas lunch in the ground floor flat. Slo' was quite the hostess and insisted that the pair of us should sit on the settee while she washed up. Then she disappeared without a word, leaving Timbers and me sitting together between the plastic Christmas tree and the tele, with a bowl of dainties in barley sugar between us.

When Timberdick asked if I remembered the first time we sat on the settee, I knew that she wanted to be sentimental. (Timbers could never be romantic. Sometimes she managed lovey-dovey but she rarely got any further.)

"You were on patrol and you found me frozen stiff in the porch of the old Methodist Hall. You lifted me onto my feet and I tricked you into bringing me back here."

"We sat here for the rest of the night," I remembered.

"Mind, you fell asleep after twenty minutes, so you don't really know what went on." Then she took a breath and said, "I'm saying that I couldn't carry on, living the way I do, if we got married. I'd have to change the things I do. I mean, for instance, working."

At that moment, Slowly manoeuvred her way through the front door. She was carrying an old portable radio with a mains lead attached and a lampshade and bulb on the top. "Don't touch!" she cried as she positioned it on a table. "Harry Ainsworth, across the road, has tuned it in and says all we've got to do is turn it on and listen."

"Oh, there was no need to ask Harry," I said. "We could have set it up."

"We're not missing this, Ned Machray. We weren't going to rely on your radio fingers. But first – your present!"

I looked at Timbers; she shrugged. She knew that we'd lost the mood. I wanted to promise that we would talk again later but Slowly was all over the place. Under the table, she plugged in the radio. From behind the settee, she put her hands on my shoulders and told me to close my eyes.

"Make sure he does,Timbers," she shouted excitedly and disappeared into the bedroom.

We heard some seasonal shuffling and crumpling of paper before she emerged from her bedroom with a large package. At first, I thought it contained the latest model locomotive but it was much larger and heavier. I tore away the paper and sliced the sellotape from the acres of ill-fitting cardboard. Then I opened the folds to reveal the missing trombone.

Slowly was kneeling in front of me. "There!" she shouted and clapped her hands. "I had it all the time. Sergeant Bernie and Alice gave it to the Admiral and he brought it to my house and nobody knew! He went and died and nobody knew!"

"What do you think of that, Timbers?" I asked, but Timbers had slipped out of the room.

"Don't worry about her, Ned. The trombone! Play the trombone!" Slowly was bouncing around and giggling, hiding her face when the excitement got too much for her.

"No. No, I couldn't. I'm not a musician. But, you know, now that I'm holding it, I can almost believe the stories. You know, it does seem to have the spirit."

The front door slammed and, outside in the cold, Timberdick's figure ran past the window. She didn't turn around as she crossed the street.

I was saying, "I can almost believe that Miller did play this. I mean, there's absolutely no proof that he didn't."

"The radio!" Slowly squealed. "We'll miss the beginning."

As I mimicked a trombonist, without making a sound, Slowly

switched on the radio.Through the crackle of an amateur pirate broadcast, we heard Sean's slightly tinny voice. "We present a Christmas concert by The Hoboken Arms' Uptown Hall Gang."

"Shh, listen," said Slowly. She sat on the floor, though really there was too much of her to be comfortable.

The music and my announcement commenced simultaneously but they had the feel of a transmission that was likely to spiral away into the ether at any moment.

"This is Alvar Liddell welcoming you to the Cafe Rouge of the Hotel Pennsylvania on the shores of Long Island Sound ...."

"My favourite introduction!" I shouted.

"I know! I know! I persuaded him! I made him do it!" She bobbed up and down, her head rocking on her shoulders. "Mind you, it bloody cost me!" She jumped up to the settee.

"We regret that Captain Glenn Miller cannot be with us this Christmas Day but we present a programme of marvellous Miller melodies ...."[6]

"It's a bloody cheat," said the young girl wheeling her new scooter along the pavement. "It looks like snow, but when you get dressed up and ready, it turns out it's not."

"Bloody right," said Timbers as she walked down Goodladies Road. "It's a bloody cheat."

Because it was Christmas Day, children had taken possession of the side streets. The next generation of mothers stood with their toy

---

[6] At Blackbush Sunday Market in the 70s, I found four unlicensed recordings of the broadcast. The 7" sleeves were plain white card wrapped in cellophane with old lingerie adverts cut crudely to size and inserted to make do for a cover. An over-printed label, 'from Lady Brenda's Music Stores' made me wonder just how much the Chief Constable's wife had to do with the project. Then I remembered that old man McKinley had written the original provenance on the back of an old lingerie advert, and my way forward was clear. I had to collect every copy of the bootleg and, sooner or later, I would come across the definitive history of the Twinwood Trombone.

prams on the corner of Rossington Street and complained, very grown-up, about the peculiar little ways of each of their dolls. The lads wanted to get a soccer game going, but there were too many new balls, and too many new strips that had to be worn, first time out, by centre forwards. Barry Butler, who knew that he wanted to be a goalie and nothing else, stood at the railway arches and tried to keep warm while the pecking order was argued. Others, just too young to be called teenagers, posed on doorsteps and against lamp-posts, determined to say very little, but hoping that others would admire the best presents that they had brought out of doors. Mrs Hawkins had no children but enjoyed each Christmas Day better than the last. She sat on her doorstep and watched it all.

"The photograph!" Soapy shouted as he tried to hurry across the road. He was rosy cheeked and wobbly on his feet. "I've got three copies. I know, they're already wet, what with the snow and rain. But they're great, Timbers. Who took it?"

"Ned's old-time nurse," she replied without slowing down, wanting to hide her face.

"They're bloody good, Timbers!" he shouted, four or five steps behind.

"Not now, Soapy."

"You've got nothing on and just Glenn Miller's trombone to cover you up."

The pictures showed Timberdick in her birthday suit. She had her back to the camera and was looking over her shoulder. Her back was pale and her shoulders bony and, when Soapy looked closely, he could see pimples between them. But it was her bottom that he wanted to see, not her spots. It was bare, like the rest of her, but it wasn't on show. Timberdick had it covered with the Twinwood Trombone. "Timbers, you must have known where it was all along," he said.

He grabbed her arm, "Hey, what's this? Tears?"

"Not now, Soapy," she said again.

"I don't understand, Timbers. Come on, we'll both go to Ma's."

"No, not like this."

He got in front of her and stopped her running. "But the trombone, Timbs. Why didn't you say?"

"Because I wanted to give it to Ned for Christmas, with my own copy of the picture."

Now, he was really puzzled. "Why didn't you?"

She pulled herself away from him and ran down Chestnut Alley.

"Another day, then," he said, standing still and knowing that she wouldn't hear. "I'll get you to autograph the pictures on another day."

THE TIMBERDICK MYSTERIES

"Noble has a fine knack of creating a sense of place and atmosphere. He has created an intriguing set of characters."

Portsmouth Post

"A marvellous creation. Noble reels off a first rate story. Vastly entertaining."

Nottingham Post

"He leaves you begging for the next in the series."

Montgomeryshire Advertiser

TIMBERDICK'S FIRST CASE
Matador Paperback
ISBN 1-904744-33-8

Timberdick worked the pavements of Goodladies Road where the men had bad ideas and the girls should have known better. In 1963, the murder of a prostitute challenges more than Timbers' detective skills. "Real people get murdered by their family and friends," says one of the girls. "We get killed by everyone else."

LIKING GOOD JAZZ
Matador Paperback
ISBN 1-904744-96-6

Searching for an abandoned infant, Timberdick learns that the father has been murdered. She can trust no-one, not even those who are close to her. Before it's all over, she's sure of only one thing. No place rocks like the Hoboken Arms on Tuesday night!

PIGGY TUCKER'S POISON
Matador Paperback
ISBN 1-904-905237-18-9

Timberdick is back! She's living in the vestry and working nights in the Curiosity Shop when a stranger is murdered at the top of the stairs. Timbers is arrested but she has no time to waste in a police cell. She has a murder to solve and a bun in the oven.

THE CASE OF THE DIRTY VERGER
Matador Paperback
ISBN 978-1905886-319

It's 1947 but there's still no peace on Goodladies Road. Men without a war and girls without homes is a cocktail for murder. We explore Timberdick's first nights on Goodladies Road and find clues to many of the characters that we have already met in her later cases.

THE PARISH OF FRAYED ENDS
Matador Paperback
ISBN: 978-1906221-799

When the Chief Constable asks questions about a superintendent who was buried two years ago, our street-wise detective finds that she is investigating three murders instead of one. But three suspects say that they were in bed with her favourite policeman on the night of the murder, so Timbers can see only one way forward. She sets a date for her wedding.

A MYSTERY OF CROSS WOMEN
Matador Paperback
ISBN 978-1848760-929

In 1937, Ned Machray has been a policeman for only a few weeks when he finds his first murder but, in this prelude to the Timberdick Mysteries, he solves the case that has baffled Scotland Yard, Whitehall and the local CID.

THE CLUE OF THE CURATE'S CUSHION

Matador Paperback

ISBN 978-1848763-029

"I'm twice the detective you'll ever be. I already know who killed Amy Bulpit and I'm not telling you." Ned Machray knew that she was teasing. It was all part of Timberdick's game to teach him a lesson.

Keep up to date with Timberdick's website

www.bookcabin.co.uk